A FORBIDDEN PARANORMAL ROMANCE

A.E. COSBY

*For those of you who like Venom for... reasons.
This one is for you.*

AUTHOR'S NOTE

Thank you for deciding to read Death and Shadow!

While Death and Shadow is a prequel to The Chaos Series, it is recommended to be read between The Chaos Wielder and Wrath's Daughter. But that is up to you! Keep in mind that this is **not** a standalone.

This book is a beautiful romance with dark elements. Please consider the content warnings below and if any are not for you, please do not read. Your mental health matters more!

General: graphic language, graphic violence, graphic torture, mentions of suicides, mentions of murder, mentions of violence involving children, ghosts of children, mentions of child abuse, mentions of domestic violence, gaslighting, victim blaming

Romance: Orgasm denial, choking, pegging, breeding kink, cum worship, graphic sex, graphic language, teratophilia, venom-like tongue that deliciously wraps around her neck, double penetration

DEATH & SHADOW SOUNDTRACK

You can follow the Death and Shadow Soundtrack on Spotify

Music. I see the world through music. Notes fly through the air, creating song and sound for everything I see. Everything has a song. Everything has a theme. Music has always been a part of my soul. It's how I associate with life.

It was crucial for me to create a soundtrack for each of my books. Every major scene has a song. Every main character has a song. To add an interactive piece to the novel, when there's a scene with a song, you'll find * with a footnote with the name of the song to listen to.

Theme Song:
"Mine" by Sleep Token

Scene Songs:

1. "River" by Bishop Briggs
2. "Lightning Over Mexico" by Tom Morello, The Bloody Beetroots, Ana Tijoux
3. "Close" by Nick Jonas, Tove Lo
4. "Sweat" by ZAYN
5. "I Want To" by Rosenfeld
6. "Something to Hide" by grandson
7. "Romance" by Varials
8. "Heaven" by Pink Sweat$
9. "I Want It" by Two Feet
10. "Make Me Feel" by Elvis Drew
11. "Natural" by ZAYN
12. "lovely" by Billie Eilish, Khalid
13. "Like I'm Gonna Lose You" by Meghan Trainor, John Legend
14. "P*$$Y Fairy (OTW)" by Jené Aiko
15. "Heavenly Bodies - Villains Overture" by Arankai
16. "Body" by Rosenfeld
17. "Crazy in Love - Remix" by Beyoncé

PRONUNCIATION GUIDE & GLOSSARY

DEITIES

Axton (ax-tin) - Deity of Death, War, and Rebirth

Etis (e-tis) and Sortis (soar-tis) - Double headed Deity of Love and Sexuality

Gaelen (gay-len) – Deity of the Hunt

Melvina (mel-veen-ah) - Deity of Space and Time, Protector of the Abused

Tomis (toe-miss) - Deity of Chaos

ANGELS

Aeshma (a-shh-mah) - Angel of Wrath

Gabriel (gae-bree-el) – Angel of Messengers and Military

Kutiel (cute-eye-el) - Angel of Water and Divinity

Michael (mike-el) – Angel of Battle Strategy and Earth

Rhamiel (Rah-me-el) – Angel of Storms

Sarandiel (sah-ran-dee-el) - Angel of Night and Shadows

SERAPHS

Agiel (ay-g-el)- Second to Mitzrael, intelligence

Apollyon (uh-pol-yuhn) - Destroyer, Jailer

Matriel (mat-tree-el) - Overseer and head of the Iuris

Mitzrael (miz-rye-el) - Security, intelligence

Zaphkiel (saf-kye-el) - Second in command to the Overseer

DEMONS

Norrix (nor-ex) - Demon of Pain and Fear

LOCATIONS

Euhaven (you-hey-vin)

Asherai (ash-er-eye)
Calñar (cal-knee-ar)
Melhold (mel-hold)
Shayce (sh-ay-ss)
Potroya (poe-troy-ah)
Gailux (gae-lucks)
Temisraine Ocean (tem-is-rain)

REALMS

Aether (a-ther) - upper world, home to the majority of Angels, overseen by Tomis

Medius (mid-e-os) – Euhaven, home to the majority of mortals

Orcus (awr-kuhs) - underworld, home to the majority of Demons and Demies, overseen by Axton

Novus Mors (no-v-us) (more-s) – main land, capital of Orcus

Cassus (cass-yus) – the in between, limbo, anima rehabilitation, Wayward souls

Pax (packs) – the afterlife and peace, reincarnation

Mordax (more-ducks) – punishment for evil animas

Ingens (een-gens) – realm in sister galaxy

OTHER

Aethen (a-then) – common language of celestials

Anima (an-ee-mah) – soul

Celestials – Seraphs, Deities, Angels, Demons, Demies

Concilium Iuris (con-chee-lee-um) (e-you-ris) – high council of Seraphs that oversee the celestial realms.

Consiliarius (con-see-lee-ar-ee-oos) – head councilor

Demi(es) (Dem-ee) – people who are half Deity

Quasars (kw-ay-sars) – Celestial Special Forces

Sol Cycle: the orbit around Sol (the sun). Equivalent to 7 Euhaven years.

Tenura (ten-oo-rah) – Prison

ORCUS 
Novus Mors
Mordax
Orcus Proces
The Tenura
Daxurb
Malus Volcano
To Aether

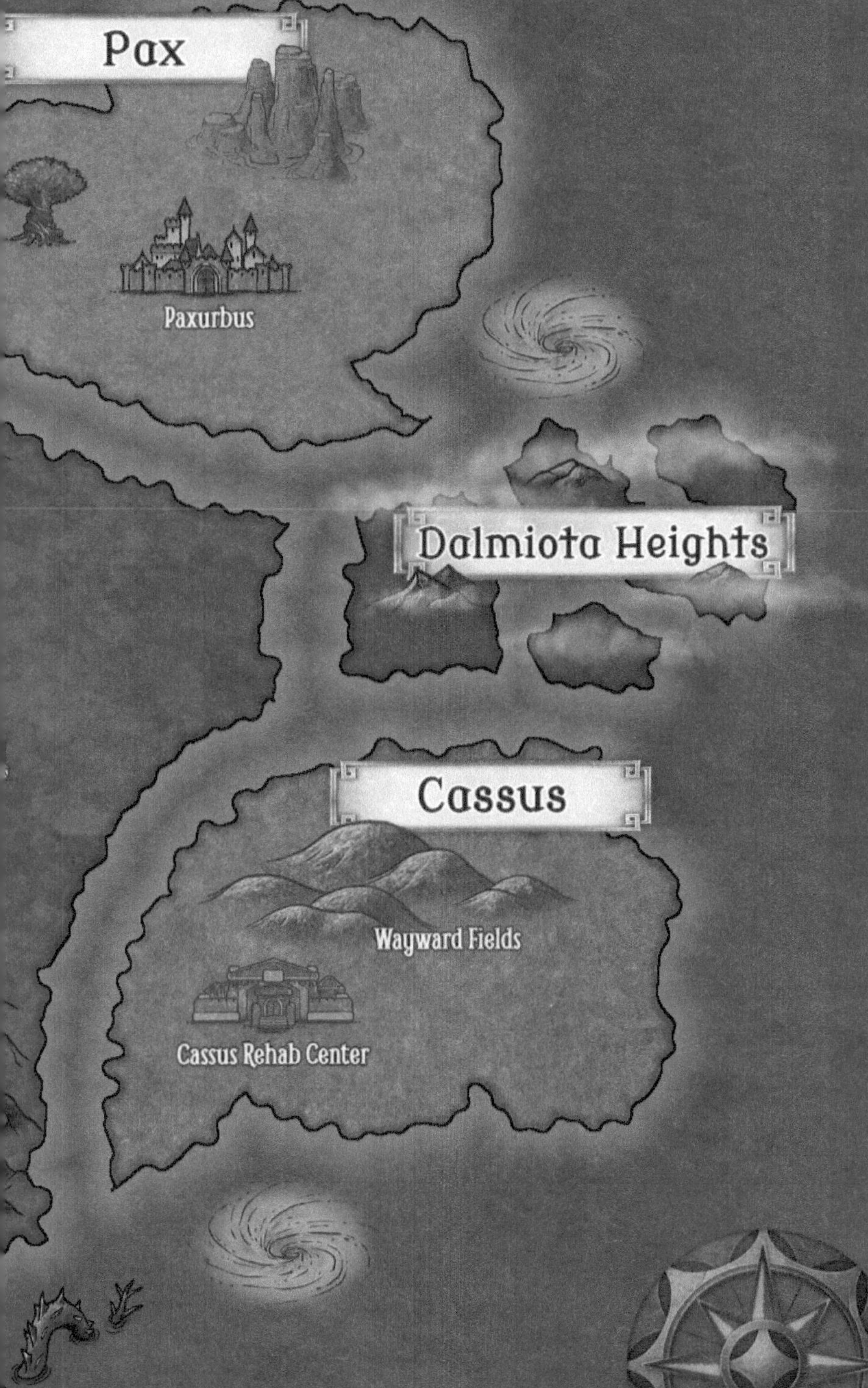

Pax
Paxurbus
Dalmiota Heights
Cassus
Wayward Fields
Cassus Rehab Center

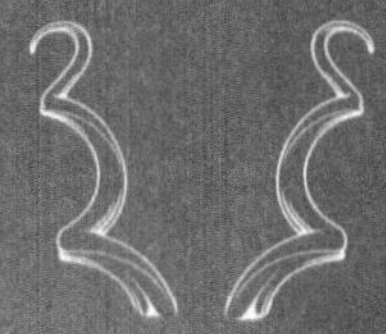

CHAPTER 1

AXTON

Three Sol cycles Before Aeshma's Escape

"**A**eshma is creating a ruckus within Medius, and we need to stop her before she attempts to escape!"

Tomis's nasally voice dug into Axton's brain, making him grind his teeth. The Deity always rubbed him the wrong way. Maybe it was the flowing hair of brilliant flame or the flurry of orange chaos she tended to surround herself with. Or maybe it was because she'd always been this annoying since they were first conceived by the Creator.

"Sister, if you do not get out of my bloody face..." He stood from his desk, glaring at her. It would be impossible for Aeshma to break free from his Ascendent, the prison that had kept the Angel caged for nearly five thousand years. "What is it that makes you think she'll break out now, huh? My Ascendents have never failed. Even the Concilium Iuris still use the ones I made for them."

"It's almost like you have not noticed the aggression on Medius, brother mine. The sudden uptick in wrath-fueled deaths? It has been getting worse over the last two Sol cycles!" She stood to pace, her black pantsuit whispering as she walked.

"And what? That means nothing. Only that I get more animas to process."

She turned her pure, sun bright eyes on him in fury. "This is not the time for mockery!"

"Oh, I was being deadly serious." The more animas he had, the more the power fueled him. "Euhaven has been going to shit. Again. It's bound to descend into a little chaos. You of all Deities should be happy about that." He grunted as he made his way around her. Chaos fueled Tomis the way animas fueled him. He opened his office door and motioned with a hand. "Sister, kindly remove yourself from my office before I remove you myself."

"You will come to regret this, brother. If Aeshma breaks free, she *will* destroy Medius like she nearly did so long ago." She glared at him, flaring with frustration.

"I know, sister. I was there." Axton rolled his sapphire eyes in annoyance. "To quote the mortals 'we'll cross that bridge when we get there.'" He barely gave her time to leave before slamming the door behind her and began pacing. He refused to believe that Aeshma could escape. That would mean he failed, and that Melvina sacrificed her life for nothing. No, he would not accept failure.

As he was about to sit at his desk, there was a soft knock on his door. He stalked back to it and yanked it open.

"What!"

Sarandiel stared up at him with her pure black eyes, carrying a binder in her arms, her smile bright as day.

"My apologies, love, I thought you were Tomis…" He sighed as he opened the door wider for her to enter. The scent of almond oil and coconuts wafted in the air as she walked by. The Angel was stunning. For the centuries he'd known her, he never tired of her presence. But he'd never tell her that.

"Thank the Creator that I'm not," Sarandiel chuckled.

Axton subtly took her in, enjoying the way her navy skinny jeans hugged her hips and firm legs. Her off-the-shoulder, lilac blouse dipped to show the swell of her small breasts and made her dark brown skin shine. Her silver and black braids were up in a bun, a few escaping around her face. Bracelets circled her arms, stacked halfway to her elbows. They rang like bells as she plopped the binder down on his obsidian desk.

"Fucking Orcus, what is all that?" Axton stood next to her, feeling her radiant warmth. They both moved to open the binder at the same time. His hand landed on hers and a soft shock passed between them, causing Sarandiel gasp. The sound traveled straight to his dick. Fuck. Her breathing turned shallow as he slowly glided his fingers along the back of her hand before removing it. Were her lips as soft as her skin?

Axton, focus.

Sarandiel cleared her throat as she shook off whatever she was feeling. "These are new animas. Hundreds. There is a war stirring on Medius."

"War is always brewing. Deaths are always occurring." He looked at the binder, assessing the deaths. "Murderer. Rapist. Serial killer. Trafficker." He listed as he turned a page. "This happens every day. What makes these wankers any different?"

"Wrath drove them to commit these crimes, but then they committed suicide out of guilt. These were everyday people who never had a violent bone in their body! It was as if a switch flipped and suddenly their entire personalities changed." She flipped a few pages to show him a group of children. "These kids murdered their headmistress because she told them they couldn't go to a carnival."

"This isn't the first time children have murdered." *And it wouldn't be the last.*

"I don't know. It feels off to me. The shadows whisper." She bit her lip as she concentrated, flipping through the binder some more.

Oh, what he wouldn't give to suck on that lower lip. Would she moan for him? No. Thoughts like that were improper, and not to mention, dangerous. Deities and Angels were forbidden to be together, especially without a Claiming which was rare in itself. Without a Claiming, their offspring were proven too unstable, which was reason enough for why such a coupling was illegal.

Sarandiel shook her head as she closed the binder with a snap, garnering his attention. He had to focus on the task at hand and get his mind out of the gutter.

"You seem angry, love," Axton said as he took the heavy thing.

Holy Creator, that was a lot of animas at once. Usually that only happened during wars or mass extinctions. Maybe Sarandiel was right. He leaned on the desk, watching as she played with a braid.

"I'm *worried*," she said softly. "Aeshma is known for her wrath. What's to say these aren't connected?" Letting out a sigh, she nodded to the binder with her chin. "Why do you still use paper when I created a perfectly extensive digital mainframe?" She crossed her arms as she leaned against the desk next to him.

"Habits?" Axton said with a shrug.

Sarandiel had always been the first to keep up with changing technologies across the realms. Having been the sole reason for the creation of the internet, it hadn't come as a surprise when she created the mainframe.

Sarandiel shook her head with a chuckle.

"Do you need help getting them sorted? I have another binder with their victims. I started sorting those because they're easier to weigh and assess. I can also visit Cassus. It's overflowing with all the sudden deaths. Animas are having a hard time adjusting. Might be a good idea to bring in extra support."

That was why he was grateful he had her around. In addition to how he felt about her, she made a great executive partner. He had to run his realm like a business. It needed order and structure. Each anima had an assignment. Axton and a select team of Angels and Demons reviewed them before they were processed. The evil were punished, either by him or one of his Demons in Mordax. The good were often easier to transition. Ushering them to Pax was simple enough, unless they were in denial about their death or had unfinished business. Those were the hardest and went to Cassus.

"Yes, that would be wonderful," Axton said before she nodded and turned to leave. He kept his eyes on her ass the entire time.

Fuck, he wondered what it would be like to sit it on his face.

CHAPTER 2

SARANDIEL

Sarandiel worked to catch her breath as she sparred with Kutiel. They were sparring in Aether's training center. Sarandiel wasn't as skilled a warrior as her brethren, but she wasn't weak either. Still, Kutiel laid her out on the mat, swiping her feet from under her. Sarandiel landed with a grunt, back plastered on the floor.

"What's wrong? You're distracted." Kutiel sat next to her while Sarandiel stared up at the ceiling, catching her breath, her sweat leaking on the floor.

"There's a rise in wrath-related killings and deaths. Previously kind and gentle people are murdering out of rage, and then committing suicide from guilt. Tomis is worried it's Aeshma trying to break free of the Ascendent." Sarandiel sighed, sitting up. "Axton isn't convinced, though."

Oh, Axton. She couldn't admit to Kutiel that *he* was the other reason she was distracted. She'd worked with him for hundreds of Sol cycles, and for hundreds of Sol cycles, she'd kept her desire for him in check. The back of her hand still scorched where he'd run his finger across it. She had to remind herself it was forbidden for Angels and Deities to be together. Their joint climaxes could level a realm if unchecked.

"Axton wouldn't be convinced even if it was dead in his face." Kutiel snorted at her own joke.

Smirking, Sarandiel rolled her eyes before standing. She grabbed a water bottle and guzzled it down.

"Just keep an ear to the ocean. The shadows are whispering, and I fear we might need the Chaos Wielder." Anxiety rippled through her at the thought. She hoped they would never have to call on them. The pair left the training facility to head to the cafeteria. Her stomach rumbled, reminding her she needed to fuel herself after training. "How is it that I'm starving?"

"It's because you don't eat enough Dee," Kutiel said with an exasperated sigh before grabbing a protein shake. The Angel plucked a sandwich, a bowl of fruit, and a salad, and shoved it in Sarandiel's direction. "Eat this."

"It's too much! I can do the fruit and salad. I'll eat more later."

Kutiel narrowed her gaze as the two of them sat down. Sweet Creator, the Angel wasn't going to let up. She grabbed the sandwich and bit into it. "Oh… this is good," she groaned with her mouth full.

"Eat up." Kutiel pushed a bottle of water toward her.

"Ok, *mother*." Sarandiel chuckled at Kutiel's irritated expression.

After polishing off her protein shake, the Angel said, "You know, when I think about it, the Temisraine and the creatures below have been unsettled." Kutiel bit her thumbnail in obvious thought. "Do you think Gabriel has any Quasar Rangers stationed in Medius?"

Sarandiel shook her head.

"Usually, Quasars don't work missions on Medius. But it would likely benefit us if we had people down there. Even if we can't directly interfere. I'll ask Axton," she said before finishing her sandwich and moving to the fruit.

Kutiel's expression soured at the Deity's name.

"All right. We'll see if good ol' Axie will do something productive."

"Don't call him that," Sarandiel snapped, suddenly defensive. She cleared her throat. "I mean… Show some respect. I'm sure he doesn't like that you all call him that."

Kutiel rolled her eyes as Sarandiel stood. "Where are you off to?" Kutiel said as she hopped to her feet, raising an eyebrow in suspicion, her tan skin glimmering in the light. It was nearly impossible to hide anything from the Angel of Divinity.

"I offered to help Axton sort the animas. There are hundreds of them." Sarandiel ignored the warning glow in Kutiel's turquoise eyes.

The Angel crossed her muscled arms, giving her a disapproving onceover. "Be safe around him. I never liked that asshole," she said with disdain.

Sarandiel fought a groan. *Everyone* had an issue with the Deity of Death. Could he be arrogant? Sure. Could he be an even bigger asshole? Of course. But she saw beyond that. Maybe they disliked him because he wasn't a boot licker.

"I've worked with him for centuries, Kutiel. Besides, I can protect myself, you know," she said with a smirk before exiting and making her way to the lift.

As she stepped into the all-glass elevator, she looked over Aether's capital. The jade sky had darkened as night approached, pale blue clouds floating across with sparks of yellow lightning occasionally making its way through. Angels flew past, on their way to Creator knew where, other denizens crossed streets far below. The elevator dinged as she arrived at the topmost floor of the Tower.

The hall of portals opened before her, each arch leading the way to different locations and realms. Per usual, the Aether Hub was busy as high-ranking individuals made their way in and out of gateways. Some required retinal scans to more secure locations. It took the various Councils ages before they would agree with Sarandiel's advice to install them. Technology was a passion of hers, and she found it more useful than her brethren gave it credit for.

Deities are lucky they can phase, Sarandiel thought to herself with a sigh.

After having her retina scanned, she stepped through the bright gateway that took her to Novus Mors. She came out on the other end of the portal hall to the compound's peacefulness.

The compound housed the immediately essential Celestials necessary to make the anima sorting process run smoothly. Outside of the compound was Novus Mors, a bustling city. One of many in Orcus. Three moons, lilac, gray, and red, shined across the horizon. Orcus's wide ring arched above in crystalline rainbow colors. The realms, or planets as they called it on Medius, stood out in the deep violet sky. Euhaven spun brightly in the distance with its moon a mere speck orbiting around it.

Lost in thought, Sarandiel made her way to her apartment. With her eyes on the floor, she bumped into a wall of muscle. She peered up at Axton, who seemed to have been waiting for her.

At well over six feet tall, Sarandiel was not a short Angel. Others often came to her shoulder or chin. Axton, however, made her feel small with his towering height. His glacial skin glimmered under the lights; bright sapphire flames lit in his eyes. His black curling horns made him seem taller as they reached toward the ceiling, silver etchings of Deity symbols shining. His recently cut navy hair was styled in short waves. She missed the way it used to flow to his waist.

She appreciated the way his black button up clung to his body, and how the veins on his forearms protruded with his hands stuffed in the pockets of his white slacks. He was delicious in every way, but she could only admire from a distance.

"Sarandiel?" The bass of Axton's voice drew her out of her thoughts, and she realized she had been staring. She quickly averted her eyes.

"Ah, I'm sorry. What did you say?"

"I asked if you were okay. You looked a bit outta sorts." His gaze bore into her.

Did he notice how she felt? How she thought of all the ways she'd fuck him if she could? Heat crept up her face and she hoped he couldn't tell.

"Yes, sorry. I just got back from sparring with Kutiel. My back met the floor quite a few times," Sarandiel chuckled, suddenly aware that she must smell of sweat and the gym. "If you don't mind waiting, I'd like to take a quick shower. I didn't expect you so soon."

"Sure thing. I can wait." Axton didn't seem annoyed or unhappy. He just leaned against the wall and crossed his arms. Stone-faced as usual.

She took in his wide lips and his clean-shaven, strong jawline. What would it feel like to be kissed by him?

"Would you rather wait inside?" she blurted out. Oh, why did she do that? "I mean, the couch is probably more comfortable than the wall." He seemed to think on it, brows creasing slightly, hesitant. "Sorry, that's improper. I'll be quick." As she opened the door, Axton grasped her wrist. His entire hand wrapped around it and sent shivers down her spine.

"It's quite all right, love. I can wait inside. Take your time," he said before letting her go and following her in.

She flicked on the lights, the living room coming to life. It was warm with tan walls, turquoise plush couches, and dark brown carpets. A mahogany coffee table sat in the middle of the room, bio-luminescent lilies overflowing a vase on top. Over by the floor length windows were three holoscreens and a holoport on her massive tech desk.

Anxiety pulled Sarandiel taut. The living room felt small with Axton taking up space. His energy was all encompassing, drawing her in. It wasn't as if they hadn't been around each other alone. They kept it cordial and professional.

Somehow, things changed over the last few decades. Quick glances became longer. They accidentally touched each other often. She felt like she was exaggerating things. It was likely not at all what she thought, just her libido craving what it hadn't had in a very long time.

"I'll be back," she said softly. She could barely breathe with him so close.

Axton gave her a long assessing look. His eyes raked over every inch of her and flared. Fuck. He could probably smell her arousal.

"Like I said. Take your time," Axton rumbled before sitting on the couch.

Sarandiel's heart thudded in her throat as she turned for her room. She had to make sure she took a cold shower.

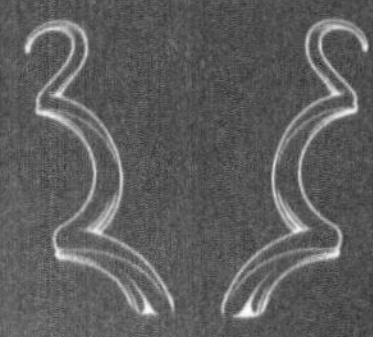

CHAPTER 3

AXTON

Why did he agree to wait inside Sarandiel's flat? He knew better than that. Her scent was everywhere. Seeing her all sweaty made his dick twitch. Fuck, he was setting himself up. He hadn't believed she wanted him due to her general lack of arousal around him. But the way she eye-fucked him just moments ago had him second guessing. Did she want him as badly as he wanted her?

"Bollocks…" he murmured to himself as he stood to pace.

Axton turned his head toward her room when he heard the shower turn off. He could imagine Sarandiel toweling off her thick thighs and round ass before working up to her breasts and back. He bit his lip to suppress a groan at the thought.

"Axton?" came her voice. He moved quickly to her door and cursed himself for his excitement.

"Yes?" he said fighting back the thoughts of her naked body hardening his cock.

"Sorry to bother you, but I have a new bottle of oil on the table that I forgot to grab. Can you pass it to me?"

Axton nearly groaned as he grabbed the oil. He couldn't help imaging her oiling up and had to adjust himself before knocking on her door. Sarandiel opened it a smidge and her clean scent wafted out. The groan slipped out of his mouth before he could stop it. Her eyes widened as she looked up at him, full lips parted slightly.

There. He caught the scent of her arousal. He knew he shouldn't, but he wanted to see if he could make her unravel.

He leaned his forearm on the doorframe above her head as he held up the oil with his free hand.

"Need this?" His already bassy voice deepened.

She visibly gulped before nodding. A smile slowly grew on his face as she attempted to take the oil from him while also trying to keep her towel around her body. "Ah ah. Say please."

Sarandiel's eyes narrowed. He stepped close enough to feel her body heat. She took a few deep breaths, wrangling herself.

"Please," she said while keeping her gaze on him.

Fuck, she was going to ruin him. Axton had always been drawn to her, but he denied himself out of duty and responsibility. Her gaze dropped to his lips as he licked them before flicking back up. He found himself leaning closer, body thrumming with the need to touch her. Sarandiel seemed to lean in before shaking her head.

"Axton. Please," she said more firmly. The sound of her voice brought him out of his trance.

"Apologies, here," he murmured as he handed her the bottle, their fingers briefly touching.

"Thanks…" she said softly before closing the door.

"Bloody Orcus," he grunted, as he moved back to the living room. "Stop thinking with your dick, Axton."

Sarandiel spent the rest of the evening helping Axton sort anima assignments. He kept stealing glances at her, admiring her beauty.

"I think this group is ready for Pax." She patted a stack on the conference desk. Binders and folders were neatly placed on the table.

He looked at each pile that covered the table, some higher than others.

"The Cassus assignments are almost equal in number to Mordax," Axton said to himself, separating them by cause of death. He had a compelling need for order. It was more than separating by realm. It had to be broken down to the finest details for the processing of animas to flow. "Even during war, Cassus assignments were never this high."

"It's because they're dying suddenly by people they thought

they could trust. I think it's easy to deny you've died because of someone you loved," Sarandiel said, quickly catching on to the next phase of his sorting, and separated the others by cause of death. "I set up an algorithm in the mainframe to capture similar assignments." She leveled a stare at him with a small smirk playing on her full lips. "Would you like the report in paper, old man?"

He snorted, caught off guard by her joke.

"That would be lovely," he said before nodding to the two remaining stacks. "Mordax. The worst of the wankers." He gave a tired sigh, undoing a button at his collar.

She eyed him. "You need rest."

"Ever the caretaker." Axton smirked as he turned to her.

"Caretaker?" Sarandiel raised an eyebrow in confusion.

"You've always looked out for me. Made sure I ate, handed off the easier assignments, to make time to go for a fly." He took a step toward her. What was he doing?

"Oh. I just..."

"You pay attention," he murmured as he took another step.

"I do."

"Indeed, you do, love. A lot." And another step. Axton found himself close enough to touch her if he wanted.

"Yes." Sarandiel cleared her throat, looking away from the intensity of his gaze.

He took a risk and placed a finger under her chin to lift her black eyes to his. "You care. Not many people notice whether I live, die, sleep or eat." He watched as the color of her cheeks deepened and a smirk pulled his lips up.

Gently, she put a hand on his forearm. "Axton, you need rest," she said softly, breathing unsteadily.

Slowly dropping his hand, he took a step back. "Right. Of course, you're right. I will see you tomorrow." He gave her a nod and phased to his penthouse.

Axton grunted as he paced his bedroom, wondering why he touched her. They could get away with it if it was an accident. Doing it on purpose meant something entirely different. Fuck, he screwed up.

"Axton you're a bloody bellend, mate," he muttered as he took his clothes off. He needed a cold shower. He stopped short, grabbing his shirt and noticing her scent.

"Shit..." he groaned, dick hardening.

What would she feel like around him? Would she fit like a glove? Would her skin glisten with sweat while he fucked her into tomorrow?

He gripped his throbbing length, imagining that it was her hand. Spitting on it, he slowly stroked, wondering what her mouth would feel around the head. Her beautiful, lush lips sucking him in, hitting the back of her throat. Would she watch him as she did it? Fucking Creator above. He stroked himself quicker, pre-cum leaking.

"What would you taste like, Sarandiel?" Axton moaned as his free hand found the wall and he leaned over.

Sweet. She must taste as sweet as she smelled. The orgasm started at the base of his spine, inching him closer to the edge. His hips jerked as he pumped himself faster. He pictured her on top, riding his cock and screaming his name.

"Fuck!" he growled as he came, painting the wall with his cerulean come. He leaned his forehead on the wall.

She was going to be the death of him.

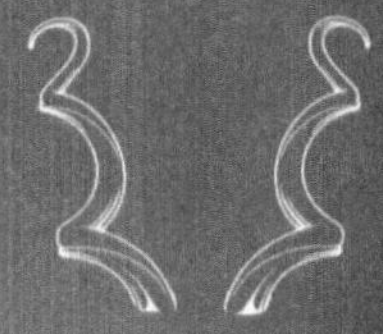

CHAPTER 4

AXTON

Axton blew out a breath as he made his way to the anima processing wing. With the sudden rise of deaths on Medius, he had been working overtime to make sure the animas didn't linger. The longer they were left in processing, the harder it would be for them to move on. He rubbed his face and sighed. He didn't want to believe that Aeshma would escape. Could he be in denial?

"M'lord…" a soft masculine voice sounded. He looked down to find a young Demon he hadn't seen before. "I was assigned to help you with anima processing."

"What is your name? This is the first time I'm meeting you," Axton said. The Demon's yellow eyes widened, pale ivory cheeks flushing red as he tried not to drop the holoport in his hand. Axton tried not to roll his eyes. The young ones always responded to him like this.

"Sorry! Gren. My name is Gren. I'm an intern." The Demon ran a hand through his short, wavy violet hair. Axton nodded to the holoport Gren held.

"What assignments did you receive?"

"Punishments on Mordax." The Demon shifted his weight, clearly uncomfortable. Axton took the device from Gren, clicking a few assignments and handing it back.

"Do Cassus. I'll have one of the upper-level Demons take care of the punishments," he said gently.

Gren nodded in gratitude before giving a bow and taking his leave.

"Why do they always give the interns the hard jobs?" he murmured to himself as he continued.

He fixed his indigo button up and black vest as he approached the Pax processing area. Each room was labeled with the subject of the assignment and difficulty level. Axton saw to it that he processed the difficult assignments to Pax. They needed the most care. He stopped short of a red alert door. 'Siblings, Murder by Parent'.

Fuck. He pulled the holoport, reading about their deaths. One was seventeen Euhaven years and the other ten. So young.

Drawing in his horns, he took a deep breath before entering the room. The soothing room had pale yellow walls and chestnut carpeting. Sunflowers played along the edges. Axton gave the brothers a warm smile. The older of the two looked up from the comfortable cream couch, holding his younger brother's hand. Earth Wieldermarks almost covered the entirety of the older brother's arm while the younger had Wieldermarks to his elbow. They wore soft gray scrubs, the standard for Pax animas.

"Hello there Jaylen and Ryder." He sat before them on a worn recliner, leaning forward to rest his elbows on his knees.

Jaylen, the oldest, wrapped an arm around Ryder's shoulders protectively.

"Why are we here?" His voice was deeper than Axton expected.

"What do you remember before arriving here?" Shit. The ones without memory of dying were the hardest.

The brothers looked at each other, communicating with their eyes before turning back to him.

"Our mom..." Jaylen cleared his throat. "Our parents were having an argument. Mom found out that dad had been cheating on her." His jaw clenched, his eyes flashing with anger.

"I don't think we were meant to, but we heard the whole thing," Ryder said sadly. "We were on the second story, listening at the top of the stairs. Dad smacked her in anger. He's *never* angry."

"I couldn't believe he even cheated on her," Jaylen continued. "I ran down the stairs as soon as I heard the slap and confronted him. He was so furious he backhanded me." He raised a hand to his cheek, though the bruise was no longer there. There was a look of shock on his face. "He hit me," his voice broke. "I was in too much shock to even think about what it meant. Before I knew it, I reacted." Jaylen's hands clenched and relaxed, voice going distant as he said, "I punched him back." The boy shuddered, anima flittering briefly like a blinking light.

"And *then* our mom got angrier. Yelling 'first you sleep with someone else and now you hit our son.' I had never heard her yell like that before." Tears traveled down Ryder's face as sorrow overtook him. "The house shook. One of them was Wielding, but everything was so chaotic we couldn't figure out who."

Axton remained quiet as he listened to their story. Talking was the only way to process what they went through.

"I was full on fighting my dad then. I couldn't let him try to abuse my mom. What if he tried to turn the anger on Ryder?" Jaylen huffed. "He ended up getting me in a chokehold. It hurt. So. Much." He rubbed his neck. "My mother was trying to pull him off me and suddenly a root sprang up from the ground and..."

"It went through mom..." the younger brother whispered. Jaylen hugged him as Ryder buried his face into the crook of his arm.

Axton ground his teeth at the thought of what these boys went through.

"I don't know why our dad did it. He seemed to have lost all sense. Then the ground shook again and more roots broke through the ground. He had them aimed at me and Ryder jumped in front..." Realization dawned on the eldest's face. "No way..." he murmured.

"What? What is it?" Ryder sniffled.

Their pain, turmoil, confusion, and anger tugged at Axton's heart. He always felt the emotions of his animas.

The younger sat up straight. "Did we die?" he gasped.

Axton gave a tight nod.

"Unfortunately, yes," Axton said.

Jaylen burst from the couch to pace.

"What? No... He couldn't have gone through with it. Why would he kill us?" Jaylen gripped his ebony hair tightly, his body going semi-translucent.

"Jaylen…" Ryder whispered. His brother continued to pace, spiraling.

"I mean, yes, he was angry. But to go as far as hurting us in that way?" He shook his head, body turning static as if watching through an old, busted HoloTV.

Shit.

"Jaylen, stop," Axton said sternly. The boy stopped in his tracks, turning to look at him. "Take a look at yourself." He yelped, horrified at what he saw. "If you don't ease yourself, you will end up on Cassus. And you don't want to go to there, right?"

The boy shook his head.

"What about our mom? She was stabbed too. Shouldn't she be here?" Jaylen asked as he sat down, his body returning to normal. Tears streamed down his face and Axton could feel the tightness in the boy's chest as if it was his own.

"Boys, your mum survived."

They looked at each other with a mixture of heartbreak and relief.

Jaylen's hands shook as he asked, "But our father. Was he arrested?"

"He ended his life in the process of hurting you both." Axton hid a grimace. A wrathful murder followed by a suicide of regret. Fuck. "He is on Mordax. He'll be there a long time before going to Cassus."

"What? He… died?" Ryder whispered, gripping his brother's arm. The young boy's body flitted as shock and sadness filled him. Jaylen stared at Axton, those waves of emotions churning through his eyes. Finally, it settled on intense mixture of grief and anger.

"He killed himself?" When Axton nodded curtly, the boy let out a wordless yell. "I know he wasn't himself when he did those things. I know it." He sobbed as he pulled at his hair. "But it makes me angry that he decided to take the easy way out instead of facing what he did!" Ryder let out a sob, holding his hands to his mouth while Jaylen continued, "Our mom is *alone* now! She has no one." Jaylen's voice went hoarse as he started to come down from the wave.

Ryder's sobs subsided as he wiped them and sat up straighter.

"She's not alone, Jaylen. She has auntie." The youngest said soothingly to his brother.

Axton was surprised at his maturity. Not many animas his age handled death well. Axton suspected it wasn't his first incarnation. Ryder nodded rapidly, gripping his brother's hand.

"I miss her already," he choked out.

"Me too..." The boy turned his attention on Axton. "So, if we're dead, what's next?" Ryder asked softly.

"I'm going to help you transition to Pax if you're ready."

"What's it like?" Jaylen gripped his brother's hand tighter.

Axton's heart felt heavy. No matter how many times he processed animas, it always left a mark.

"How about I show you?" Axton held out his hands.

Hesitant at first, the boys took hold so that he could phase them to Pax.

CHAPTER 5
SARANDIEL

A soft knock on her office door brought Sarandiel out of the holoscreen of assignments she was studying. Hologlasses covered her face as she worked through them, pulling the reports from the algorithm she set up. She looked for more commonalities between the deaths and found that most happened in waves.

Clicking the comm at her temple, the hologlasses shut off. She rubbed her eyes as she went to answer the door. Axton stood on the other side, flaming eyes dimmer than usual. His horns had been retracted and his hair looked disheveled, as if he had run his hands through it several times. Concern grew in her gut.

"Hello…" he said softly.

"Are you okay?" She had the sudden urge to reach out and give him a hug, but that would be improper.

"Yes. No. Maybe? Can we go somewhere?"

He seemed so sad. Sarandiel stared at him a moment, contemplating an answer. They had never spent any time alone together outside of the compound or council meetings. Was it a good idea to go out?

Relax, Sarandiel. It's not like it's a date.

"I'm sorry, love. Maybe it's not the best idea. I apologize for bothering you," Axton said, mistaking her silence as an answer.

"Would you like to go to Hollows?" she blurted out, wondering if the bar was a good choice. It was incredibly informal.

Shit. Maybe she should've recommended Aurora's. It held a more professional atmosphere. As she mused to herself, she felt that Axton's answer would shift something between them. They were on the cusp and a single push could change everything.

"Sure." His rich bass drew her out of her thoughts, and she could feel her heart in her throat.

Why was she so nervous? *Oh, only because you've wanted this Deity for centuries.*

The one block walk to Hollows was brisk with the cool evening air blowing around them. Hollows was cozy and warm, jazz music playing softly. The bartender nodded to them as they made their way to a booth. The worn brown leather seats groaned as they sat.

After giving their orders to the server, Sarandiel looked Axton over. "So, tell me. What has you so downcast?"

Axton leaned back, heaving a sigh. He ran a hand through his navy hair, his horns still hidden.

"There were these two boys I processed for Pax. Brothers." He rubbed a hand over his face. Sarandiel sat in silence, hiding her surprise. The Deity never spoke about his assignments, even though she was aware that he took all the hardest ones. "Their deaths fit within your theory." She raised an eyebrow in question. "Wrathful murder followed by a suicide."

"Oh no..." she gasped.

Axton proceeded to tell her about the assignment. By the end she was crying softly. Never had she known how deeply impacted he was by his assignments. It amazed her that he'd carried this for centuries.

"With all the rising deaths, it has gradually taken more of a toll." He nodded at the server as she placed a bowl of cheese fries and their drinks between them. Plucking a fry, he chewed it thoughtfully. It was cute how the Deity of Death and War enjoyed comforting fried food.

"It's a burden I didn't know you had. Is there anything I can do to help?" Sarandiel said before taking a few fries for herself. She nearly moaned at the taste of the beef brisket and cheese sauce.

"I've never spoken to anyone about it. It has always been my burden as Dominion of this Realm. It felt unfair to put that on someone else." He took a sip of his gin before picking up another fry. "Honestly, just telling you has helped," he said in between bites and licking his fingers.

She tried hard not to stare. His tongue was navy. Navy! How had she never noticed before? *Because you don't go staring into random Deities mouths.* Sarandiel fought the need to roll her eyes at herself. Her mind went to her apartment, him holding the oil, and his magnetic pull. What would it be like to have his tongue on her body?

"Plus, the comfort food," he chuckled, pulling her mind out the gutter. She could see that his flames were brighter.

"Comfort food is always a plus." She smirked, sipping her whiskey sour to wash down the delicious fries. Though it wasn't supposed to be, it felt like a date. It warmed her, and she pretended in the moment that dating Axton could be a possibility instead of illegal. "Tell me, why haven't I seen you with anyone over the centuries? Was there no one to settle with?"

"No one was ever worth the time." Axton shrugged. "I've been with plenty of mortals, of all genders. I've managed to keep the number of Demies I've fathered to a minimum." He cringed.

"Are any of them still alive?" Though rare and hard to kill, all Demies eventually died.

He let out an exhale.

"One. He's a real piece of work who gives me a run for my money. He doesn't listen very well. I want him to eventually take over for a while. So I can go on holiday for an extended period. Even a Deity needs a break. Being a Demi of a major Deity makes him different than most. His Deity half is substantially more powerful than his mortal side. His lifespan is lengthened considerably." He looked to the wall, thoughts processing across his features.

"And I take it he doesn't want any part of it?" she guessed.

"None of it whatsoever. He feels as though I abandoned him and his mother. Perhaps I did. Demies weren't as widely accepted back then as they are now. I had to prioritize my work here in Orcus. The time difference hasn't helped. One Sol cycle is seven Medius years. I never had the chance to tell him." She nodded, features schooled to understanding rather than sympathy that could be mistaken for pity. One Sol cycle was seven Medius years. It was a long time for misunderstanding to fester. "Ah, well... No use trying to talk to him at this point," he grunted, stuffing a few more fries in his mouth. "Perhaps he'll come around if he lets me explain about his mother."

Part of her grew jealous and she didn't understand why.

"Oh…" she said softly.

"Does that bother you?" Axton hedged, horns now emerging to their full glory.

A new definition of horny. She almost snorted at her own joke. A smile grew on Axton's face. Oh Creator, his smile.

"Well. Ah. Anyway. No, it doesn't," she said. Was it the whiskey making her feel hot? She grabbed some fries to try to avoid having to speak. Damn, the basket was almost empty.

"If it helps, my Demi is well over five hundred Euhaven years. His mother has long passed." He laughed at her sigh of relief. Fuck, busted. "I had a feeling you were jealous, but for what, I wonder…"

She rolled her eyes, catching some cheese that dripped from her chin. Axton reached out, wiping it off with his thumb. Sarandiel froze as he pulled back and slowly licked it off his finger. What was happening? Since when was licking cheese attractive?

"Well, you asked me about my past. What about you? Tell me, did you always want to work on Orcus?"

"To be honest?" she asked. He nodded for her to continue. "No."

He snorted.

"Stop! No. I didn't. I was perfectly content on Medius, helping Melvina with the mortals."

They protected individuals who were subjected to abuse. The thought of the Deity made her chest tighten. Melvina's sacrifice was something Sarandiel never fully got over. It didn't matter how long it'd been, it still hurt to think about.

"It was exhilarating working in the shadows, watching her use the night and celestial happenings to empower them. We're the reason that there are myths about how what goes around, comes around. Watching mortals live their small lifespans was intriguing. Rhamiel and Michael often came with us." She snapped her mouth shut.

"Michael?" Axton's tone sharpened. Being a Captain in Axton's Guard at the time, he shouldn't have been on Medius without permission.

"He's my ex," she muttered. "He felt the need to make sure I was ok during assignments." Sarandiel could feel her face getting hot, this time with embarrassment and shame. "He'd tell me what *he* would do so I followed his advice. I always ended up hurt and assumed it was because I was doing it wrong." She sighed, looking down at the napkin she was shredding into pieces. "He's the reason I left Medius. I felt like a failure. He led me to believe that I was better off at home." She pushed a braid behind her ear, bracelets twinkling as they shifted down her forearm.

A deep growl vibrated the table. Her eyes snapped up to him.

"What. Is. That?" His eyes were locked on the scar around her wrist.

Oh shit. She placed her hand on the table, the bracelets clinking back in place. Fuck, she had been careless! She knew better than to let them shift around others.

"Nothing." She gasped when Axton grasped her hand, pushing the bracelets back up. The ropelike scar encircled her wrist, no more than a quarter of an inch wide.

"This is not 'nothing', Sarandiel." His voice dropped an octave. "Did *he* do this? Did he try to Claim you against your will?"

Tears lined her eyes as she snatched her hand back and rubbed the familiar scar that represented a failed Claiming attempt.

"Claiming is supposed to happen between two animas, right?" She started ranting, anger fueling her. "The anima wants what it wants. But sometimes, one anima wants it and the other doesn't. And he couldn't accept the fact that my anima didn't want his. So yes. He tried to Claim me anyway."

Her nose flared as she took deep breaths. Forcing a Claim on an unwilling anima was equivalent to rape, and illegal. When caught, the perpetrator was thrown in an Ascendent for punishment before they died, and to the Tenura after.

"Why didn't you report him to me? Or to Melvina?" Axton

asked through clenched teeth.

She was surprised at his response, his anger. Why did he care so much?

"Me, a civilian Angel at the time, telling the Deities that one of their *Captains* tried to Claim me against my will?" Sarandiel snorted and rolled her eyes. "Doesn't work like that, Axton. Plus, you know that the scar only proves that a forced Claim was attempted, not *who* did it. It was my word against his." She sighed, ready to finish the conversation. "It happened over seven hundred Sol cycles ago. It's over."

She polished off her drink, appreciating the warmth in her belly. She wasn't going to tell the Deity that Michael had continued harassing her over the centuries.

Axton's expression softened, motioning to the server for another round. She happily grabbed the whiskey sour and took a gulp.

"What led you to Orcus?" he asked.

"You," she said quickly and winced. Fuck, didn't that sound eager.

Axton looked at her with surprise.

"Oh really? How so?" The interest in his eyes made her stomach churn. He was going to think her so silly.

"During the Civil War, you needed help with the overflow of animas. You took every step possible to make sure that Orcus still ran as smoothly as it could *while* leading the Celestial Legion. I found it admirable. I jumped on the opportunity to assist in any way I could." She turned back to fiddling with her napkin. "The first time I met you, I am sure that was when my life changed," she whispered. "You were everything that *he* was not. You showed me respect. You listened to my feedback. You showed genuine interest in what I had to say." Sarandiel pursed her lips as she thought about all the shit she'd just blurted out.

"Look at me, love," Axton said gently.

She refused, too embarrassed.

"Sarandiel, look at me," he said more firmly. Her eyes drifted up to his. He was staring at her intensely, making her hold her breath.

"Would you be surprised to know that my life, too, was changed the moment we met?"

She let out an exhale with a shuddering laugh.

"No way." Shaking her head, she took another gulp of her drink.

"Absolutely. I created Aeshma's Ascendent because of your advice. I originally thought we'd be able to take her down without needing one."

"What? Really?" she said in shock.

"Yes, really. Sarandiel, your presence calms me. I was ready to let Medius go, even if it ended me. Let the Creator make a new world if they so desired. I was through and exhausted. You are brilliant and equally as strategic. You see things that I miss and you're humble about it when you tell me. I've always respected you. I admire you. Sarandiel, I don't think you realize how much value you bring to the table… or to me." His sapphire gaze bore into her, making her stomach light up with butterflies.

"I had no idea…" She was at a loss for words.

He admired her? He found her valuable? She never would've guessed. For centuries he'd understood her, and she never knew. The bell of last call startled her and she let out a shaky sigh before standing.

"Can I walk you to your flat?" he asked as he rose next to her.

Was that a good idea? They just said some pretty heavy stuff and her emotions were running high.

"Sure."

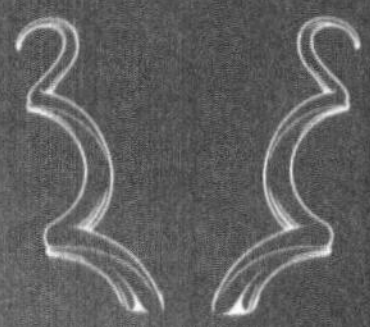

CHAPTER 6
AXTON

They decided to take a detour on the way back to the compound, making their way through the empty Nova Botanical Gardens. Axton found himself laughing as they talked about the wildest things they'd done over the centuries. Laughter felt foreign to him, and he found he enjoyed it.

"So, wait, you went skinny dipping with some shifters and then what happened?" Sarandiel was chuckling, wiping the tears of laughter from her eyes.

He shook his head, not wanting to relive the experience.

"Just know that I couldn't sit for bloody weeks."

"Oh no!" She howled, gripping his arm. Warmth spread through him. Her joy was infectious.

"Ha, ha. Yes, laugh at my embarrassment." He grinned as she pulled herself together. He plucked a nearby magenta, bioluminescent lily and faced Sarandiel. "May I?" he asked, holding the flower out. Her eyes widened as she nodded. Slowly, he glided the flower across her jaw and cheek before tucking it in her braids above her ear.

"Thank you," she said, looking up at him.

Damn, she was beautiful. Utterly beautiful. The glowing flowers surrounding them reflected off her black eyes, making them glimmer. His hand lingered, gently tracing her jaw line.

"Sarandiel…" he murmured, eyes on her full lips.

"Axton…" she said softly.

"Is it all right if I kiss you, love?"

He didn't know what made him ask. All he knew was that he needed to taste her. Find out how soft her lips were. Was he being too forward? Maybe he was. He attempted to take a step back when she caught his shirt. She pulled him in and shocked him.

"Yes."

Sarandiel raised onto the balls of her feet as he dipped his head, mindful of his horns. Their lips met in a soft caress, gentle and sweet, testing the waters. Her lips felt better than what he imagined. He licked her lower lip, making her moan softly before opening up for him. Their tongues met in a flurry, their kiss deepening. He growled, pulling her closer, his hands around her body and gliding across her soft, bare back. Her strapless maxi dress did nothing to cover her curves, and he was grateful for it.

"Wait," Sarandiel gasped, pulling away. "We shouldn't..." Her eyes were heavy lidded, lips puffy from their kiss. Her arms were around his waist, body visibly trembling as if holding herself back.

"You're right. We shouldn't," he breathed, lips close to hers. Fuck. They knew it was prohibited, and yet they didn't move away from each other. "We would be at risk if we were ever caught."

It was that statement that had him finally stepping back. As much as he wanted her, he wouldn't endanger her. The repercussions for breaking the highest commandment of the Iuris were dire, being locked in a punishment Ascendent on Sol being one of them. No, the Concilium wouldn't make death easy for them.

"I..." She shook her head.

"No, finish what you were going to say," he murmured, his body feeling the loss of her warmth.

"I know this is probably a bad idea..." Sarandiel stepped toward him, resting her forehead on his sternum.

"But?" Her almond oil and coconut scent wafted up to him, making his eyes roll. He bit back a groan, willing his dick to calm down.

She turned her head up to look at him.

"I want... I want you. I know I just told you we shouldn't, but I want to anyway," she whispered.

Axton tried to swallow the sudden lump in his throat.

"I couldn't possibly risk your life." It took all of him to not take her in his arms.

"*You're* not. *I* am. I can make these decisions." She placed a hand on his cheek. "Plus, I think about you all the time. I'm drawn to you."

He placed his on hers. He couldn't believe what he was hearing.

"I feel the same way. I have for centuries." He ran his thumb across her hand. "Are you sure about this?" It was risky. Very risky. All it took was one answer and he'd lose himself in her.

"I'm sure."*

She yelped as he scooped her up and phased to her flat. His lips crashed against hers and she opened for him as his tongue found hers. He hungrily tasted her. Tilting her head back to kiss her deeper, his tongue lengthened to snake around hers and tug on it. She gasped as they parted, watching as his tongue returned to its normal size. He grinned at her.

"Oh, that's sexy," she breathed.

The scent of her arousal drove him wild. Sitting her on the plush bed, Axton settled himself between her legs, pushing the hem of her dress up to her hips. He brought his lips to the inside of her knee. She moaned softly and squeaked when he wrapped his hands below her knees and pulled her to the edge of the bed. His hands slid up to pull off her panties. Fuck, her pussy was so close and smelled so good.

'*Sweet Creator, you're a vixen,*' Axton whispered through her mind, making her gasp.

"What was... How?" Her lust filled eyes widened slightly.

"It's just another method of communication, love." He grinned at her shocked expression. "Don't worry, I can't read minds."

Axton lifted the dress over her head, exposing her beautifully naked body. Ebony nipples hardened to tight peaks on her small but round breasts. He groaned when he found her cunt dripping and waiting for him. He pulled her closer and kissed her inner thigh. She moaned as she started to writhe.

"But it's especially useful for when my mouth is preoccupied."

"Shit," the vixen breathed.

♪ "River" by Bishop Briggs

He placed a kiss on the seam of her pussy, making her hum in pleasure. He slowly parted her lips with his fingers before snaking his tongue out and finally tasting her. Her wetness overflowed in his mouth, the nectar making him see white. Axton suckled at her clit, making her whine. She lifted her hips, giving him the opportunity to thrust his tongue into her core. It lengthened, reaching deep into her.

"Oh fuck!" she moaned as he fucked her with his tongue.

Sarandiel grabbed his horns for purchase, the feeling sending sensations of pleasure to his dick. She rubbed her pussy on his lips, spreading her juices all over his mouth and chin. He growled, letting it vibrate through her. She jolted and cried out. Abruptly, he pulled away from her and chuckled at her disappointment.

"Relax, vixen."

Axton pulled the Angel to the floor, sitting her on his face. He extended and thickened his navy tongue, and groaned as she slowly sat, taking it in like a cock. *Just like that. Fuck my face,*' he spoke to her with his mind. Sarandiel moaned as she undulated and ground against his tongue. His dick ached as she took hold of his sensitive long horns.

"That feels so good. Fuck!"

Sarandiel unhinged was the most glorious thing Axton had ever seen. She threw her head back in ecstasy, silver and black braids cascading down to her hips. He growled before widening his jaw to encompass her entire pussy in his mouth. The Angel cried out as his top lip rubbed against her clit and his lower teased her asshole. Axton thrusted with his tongue as she sat and rocked. Sarandiel's legs started to shake, clenching around his face.

'Come on my face, vixen.'

She screamed suddenly, grinding against him roughly before she came. He drank down the flood of pleasure. She sat on his chest, staring down at him as he returned his jaw to normal.

"Hmmm, you taste exquisite." Axton sat up, making her slide into his lap. "One orgasm isn't enough. Do you want my dick, vixen?"

He grasped her braids, pulling her in and kissing her deeply. Axton groaned as her tongue rubbed against his. She took his lower lip between her teeth and bit down, making him hiss. Sarandiel pulled back and gazed at him with her pure black eyes.

"Yes," Sarandiel said as shadows exploded out of her. They ripped at his clothes, reducing them to shreds and leaving him bare. Shadows made their way up the course of his abs, flowing over his broad shoulders and muscular arms.

"Do you feel the sensations of your shadows?" Axton groaned as they wrapped around his firm thighs.

"I do, and you feel amazing," she said with a moan. "These are fucking hot." Her shadows flicked over the piercings in his nipples, making him growl.

Axton flipped her on her back, sucking in one of her hardened peaks. She dug her nails into his shoulders while her shadows continued to play across his body. He shuddered as they found his cock, stroking it.

"Patience, vixen," he chuckled into her breast.

"No. I've wanted you for from the moment I met you. I'm finally having you. I need you to fuck me. Please!"

Axton froze as he leaned over her. Sarandiel wanted him as much as he wanted her. They had denied each other for so long. The room quaked as he took her lips with his own. Her body trembled as the head of his cock teased the opening of her core.

"Wait," he groaned, holding on to mere threads of restraint. "When was your last heat?"

She stared up at him in amazement, as if surprised he bothered to ask.

"Four Sol cycles ago. I have another five before the next one," she whimpered into his mouth as her shadows pushed at his ass, encouraging him to penetrate her.

"Needy, aren't you?" he growled as he ran his long tongue down her neck to her breast. They both groaned as he slowly worked himself into her wet pussy. Fuck she felt so good. The Angel's eyes flared in surprise as he pulled out and slowly pushed in, widening her further.

"Oh, Creator above, you're so thick," she gasped. "You're too big."

Axton continued to take his time fitting himself into her tight cunt, watching as he did so.

"Oh fuck!" she cried as he filled her to the hilt.

"Hmm, that's right. You can take it, angel. Your pussy looks so beautiful taking my dick." Her shadows writhed in response to his praise. Axton hissed in pleasure as they pulled the piercings at his nipples. "Fuck, keep doing that." They tugged harder, making him buck with a rough grunt.

"Axton! You're my devastation."

Sarandiel raised her hips to meet his thrusts as he picked up his pace, her juices overflowing. The shadows continued to play with his nipples, pushing at his ass. Axton growled as he hooked his arms under her knees. He plunged deeper into her cunt, feeling her cervix as he did so. With each rock, Sarandiel cried out louder.

"If I'm your devastation, you're my salvation. You saved me from myself, even from a distance."

It was the truth. He fell for her the moment she begged for his help against Aeshma. Her desire to save Medius and the realms made him care because *she* cared. Her gratitude had warmed his dark heart, and her constant presence kept him sane.

A groan vibrated Axton's body against Sarandiel's as his jaw widened like a snake to wrap his mouth across her throat. His tongue massaged as he bit gently. She whimpered as he fucked her hard and deep. Her shadows traveled between his legs to massage his balls. Another slithered between his ass cheeks and he moaned.

'Fuck, vixen. You know what to do with those shadows of yours.'

"Yes. Yes, I do," Sarandiel panted a laugh before he clamped down without breaking her skin.

Her pussy gushed over his cock and down her ass, soaking the floor. The Angel clenched around him, making him see stars. She moved her hands to grip his horns as she lifted her hips to meet his deep thrusts.

"You're soaking me, vixen." Axton's voice was guttural through his wide mouth. He ran his thick tongue along her jaw. "How would it feel to have my tongue wrapped around your throat?

Would you like that?" Sliding his tongue across the sensitive flesh, he thrusted into her with a slap of his balls against her ass.

"Yes, please!" His vixen begged, her shadows writhing.

Growling, his tongue vibrated as he snaked it around her neck tightly.

"Oh fuck!" she sobbed through the hold. Her legs shook, her pussy clenching tight around his cock. Axton loosened just enough for her to take a long gasp. "I'm going to come."

He tightened his hold, slowing his thrusts into a torturous pace. She let out a desperate moan, using her shadows to push him deeper.

'How badly do you want to come, vixen?' Axton whispered into her mind.

"Ruin me!" she cried out, tears of pleasure rolling down her the sides of her face. He pulled back from her neck, his tongue swirling in the air. "Fuck." Sarandiel panted before he slid his tongue down to her swollen clit, rubbing it in circular motions.

'Come for me, angel. Flood the floor.'

He moaned as he drove into her, abusing her tight cunt. She let out a wild scream as her orgasm crashed over her, overcoming him. He continued to taste her clit as he prolonged her orgasm until she blew apart a third time. The shadows wrapped around him, pulling at his nipple piercings at the same time as they massaged his balls.

'I am going to fill your sweet pussy.'

His orgasm barreled down his spine, making him break away from her clit to let out a roar that shook the room. The force of his come overflowed from her core and poured onto the floor.

"Death. You're the death of me," Sarandiel chuckled, body shivering from pleasure.

Axton barked out a laugh, making them groan from the raw sex. He helped place her legs down, rubbing her hips to ease the aches. He retracted his jaw, tongue slowly gliding across her sensitive nipples before returning to normal. He kissed her deeply before catching her tears, tasting the salt of her pleasure.

"Well, I *am* the Lord of Death, vixen."

CHAPTER 7
SARANDIEL

Sarandiel's braids swayed in her high ponytail as she walked down the hall of gateways toward the Cassus portal. The increase of deaths filled the sub-domain faster than they could manage. Many Angels and Demons worked overtime on assignments and processing. The last time the sub-domains of Pax, Cassus, and Mordax flooded with this multitude of animas was the civil war, seven hundred and fifteen Sol cycles ago.

If there was any indication that a breakout was near, this was it. She hoped she could make Axton shift his perspective.

Heels clicking gently as she walked through the portal, Sarandiel took in the soft pastel colors of Cassus's receiving center. As with all the sub-domains, there was only one way in and out; through Novus Mors. The walls were a cornsilk, encouraging a sense of calm, while the comfortable furniture was an amalgam of rose, pale turquoise, and eggshell. That was how it was in Cassus. All vibrant colors turned pastel as soon as they passed the portal.

Celestials of all kinds moved through the space, some carrying holoports filled with their assignments for the evening.

"G'day Ms. Sarandiel," Jules's gentle, harmonic voice sounded from behind the reception desk. Her straight, lilac hair rested just above her shoulders, sea green eyes warm and soothing. She stood slowly, her cornflower dress flowing over a rounded belly.

"Hello Jules. Oh! Don't get up on my account. Please, sit. I know the little one is due soon."

The Demi sat with a gracious smile. "How are things?"

Sarandiel picked up a holoport, pulling up recently processed animas. "More denials than unfinished business." She sighed, one assignment snagging her attention. "This anima has been here for two and a half Sol cycles?" In the grand scheme of things, that was not a very long time, but it happened to be when the first animas were affected by the wrath-fueled crimes on Medius.

"Oh yes. That is Benécio." Jules frowned. "He still doesn't believe he's dead and murmurs often about seeing Angels. Which, as a mortal human from Medius, should be impossible, right?"

Sarandiel nodded tightly, taking his file. Her periwinkle romper flowed around her as she made her way down the high-risk hallway, painted in the same cornsilk as the reception area. Each room she passed held a flittering anima, either reliving their last moments before dying in denial, or Orcus-bent on finishing business they left on Medius. These were the most high-risk of going Wayward.

"Why am I here?" a wiry, high-pitched, feminine voice said in panic. "One minute I was arguing with my partner and the next I am here."

Sarandiel looked on where a Demon with seafoam hair and peach skin was helping an anima dressed in eggshell scrubs.

"Do you remember anything else?" the Demon said softly.

The woman shook her head rapidly, her body flitting see-through and back to solid.

"Just arguing. I don't even remember what we were arguing about. I just remember that we were both very angry." The anima froze, body almost completely translucent. "Wait… I remember their hand around my throat."

As soon as the words left the woman's mouth she trembled, body convulsing as if having a seizure. What? This never happened before. The Demon grasped her by the arms gently, the parts touched returning solid. As they helped the woman lay on the couch, they raised their yellow eyes to Sarandiel.

"They're all like this," the Demon's masculine alto was gentle as they knelt by the anima and brushed her hair back. Sarandiel read their name tag.

"Andi?" The Demon looked as Sarandiel said their name. "What are your pronouns?"

"They, them. Thanks for asking." Andi smiled sadly before

standing. "More and more animas are arriving with no memory of dying. When they *do* remember, they go into convulsions and then forget all over again. That isn't supposed to happen, right?"

"No, it's not. It's concerning. Is there a common denominator with them?" Sarandiel had a feeling she knew the answer.

"They've all been murdered by someone they loved. Often brutally." Andi shook their head. "I've worked here for over thirty Sol cycles. I've never seen anything of this magnitude. There were fluctuations over the last few cycles, but nothing like this." Suddenly the anima on the couch sat up with a shout.

"Where am I?" she asked, confused. "Why am I here?" She looked to Andi and then Sarandiel. "One minute I was arguing with my partner and the next I am here."

"Make sure to sort all similar assignments like this in the mainframe and keep me apprised." Sarandiel gave Andi an empathetic smile as she took her leave. Her theories were proven, and she really wished that they hadn't been. As she arrived to Benécio's room, she noticed it was empty.

"He's in the garden," said a nearby Angel.

"Thank you."

Sarandiel left the building toward the Cassus rehabilitation garden. Animas flittered about, occasionally plucking pastel-colored flowers or attempting to plant new ones. Their bodies were more corporeal, having started to come to terms with their deaths.

"Sarandiel!"

"Krista!" Sarandiel smiled at the familiar anima flitting up to her. "You're looking well."

Krista's body was completely corporeal, save for when she moved. The anima had been on Cassus for fifty Sol cycles, but instead of going Wayward like most anima that remained for that long, she held on. In her heart, she was waiting for her husband. She refused to move on until he arrived.

"I know it's sad to say, but Erik's in Novus Mors for processing! My love. My husband." Krista's smile was wide and bright. "I can finally move on to Pax once he's ready. You and the others have been so patient with me and kept me from going Wayward. I'm forever grateful for you all."

"Don't thank us, you did the work! Pax has been waiting for you." It felt odd to congratulate an anima for the death of their spouse, but it was a reunion for them both. Even in death there was love to be found and reunited. "Be blessed. I am very happy for you both."

Sarandiel tucked a wisp of blonde hair behind Krista's ear and bowed her head before seeking out her reason for visiting the garden.

"Aye Dios. No. ¡Vi los Angeles! No estoy muerto." A man, likely Benécio, paced frantically. His body was like static, hazy and wild. "No estoy muerto," he repeated to himself.

Sarandiel approached him slowly, knowing that engaging with a borderline Wayward anima had to be done with care. She pulled from the plethora of languages that she knew to recognize the Potroyan he spoke.

"Hola. ¿Eres Benécio?" she asked as she made herself known.

The man turned panic-stricken brown eyes to her. They were lined with gold around the irises, which intrigued her. She never met a human with eyes like his.

"Sí. I am Benécio. I am familiar with Aethen," he said, the panic leaking from his expression as it turned impassive. "Are you here to explain to me why I am here in Cassus and not on Euhaven?"

Sarandiel froze. Animas that were in Cassus didn't know *where* they were. Only that they weren't where they used to be. How did this human know where he was? That is when she noticed his attire. While turned pastel due to the nature of Cassus, it was clear that he wore the traditional vestment of an Asherite Monarch.

The file didn't mention he had been a Monarch. Usually, Monarchs were taken to a separate facility if they were on Cassus. Their deaths were treated very differently.

"Benécio, if you are aware you are in Cassus, then surely you understand why," Sarandiel said gently.

The Monarch sighed.

"Death. But it's impossible. I couldn't have died," he murmured, panic quickly passing across his features. "No. I saw

Angels. I have work to do, and I can't do it from here. Return me now."

"That can't be done for many reasons. One, resurrection is illegal and punishable by true death. Two, even if you were to return, there would be no body to house your anima."

"Oh, I have that handled. You worry about returning me and I'll worry about the vessel in which to place my anima."

The fact that he said it with a straight face had Sarandiel internally scratching her head. There was something very off with Benécio.

"So, you acknowledge you're dead?"

"No. To be dead is to imply I've moved on to Pax. I am not in Pax, correct?" He raised an eyebrow as he waited for her answer. The condescension in his tone lit a fire in her belly.

"You're an Alchemist, aren't you," Sarandiel said matter-of-factly and not as a question.

Alchemists always tried to extend their brief lives, and almost always ended up in Cassus first. It always surprised them when their life ended abruptly because of a failed experiment.

"And a geneticist." Benécio paced slowly. "You see, I can't be dead because I have a job to fulfill. I can't do that from here."

"Do you know how you ended up here in the first place, Monarch?" Sarandiel was usually patient with animas, but this one rubbed her the wrong way.

"Something about an explosion, I think?" Suddenly, his body convulsed and she caught him before he hit the ground. Everywhere she didn't touch, his body turned translucent and staticky. He looked up at her with a shocked expression. "What am I doing in your arms? Unhand me."

Sarandiel fought an eye roll as she let him go.

"Benécio, you're on the verge of Wayward. If you don't come to terms with your death, you won't be able to move on at all."

"No. No estoy muerto. Imposible. Vi los Angeles." He echoed his earlier statement. He rocked his head, running his hands down his light brown face, before looking at her once again. "I don't want to move on. I want to return. I saw the Angels before coming here."

"How is that possible? Angels aren't allowed to show themselves to the general population on Euhaven." She would make sure she followed up with Axton. It was clear Gabriel had to get his Quasars on this.

"Oh, she was encased. I pulled her DNA and stored it." Sarandiel blanched. "Don't worry, it's safe. But I have to return to her. Finish what I started."

"Tell me about the DNA. Where did you find it?" Her heart thudded in her throat. If he was experimenting with Angel DNA, what else were the mortals up to?

"We found this metallic cylinder. Oval in design with Deity symbols etched into it. We tried to open it, but it didn't fully work. A very minuscule crack was all we could get. But what escaped was a feather. That's when I knew what we found." The mortals had found Aeshma's Ascendent!

"Where is the cylinder? Do you have any idea *who* is in there?"

"I don't know. Can't really tell you that after being down here for so long, can I?" Fuck. He had a point. She had to get this news to Axton. Before she had the chance to ask more questions, Benécio's pacing slowed, his movements becoming stagnant.

"What is this?"

Double fuck.

"As I told you, Monarch, you're becoming Wayward. You can't return, you won't move on. You'll become frozen and just remain forever. There's no turning back from it, and you lose your chance for reincarnation. It's a true death."

"What? No! No." Panic returned to his eyes as he tried to resume his pacing. He looked over her shoulder at the rolling fields of melon-colored grass under a lilac sky. It was filled with frozen animas, stuck forever in Cassus.

"If you accept your death, you can move on." She knew she was losing the battle as his movements slowed further and his speech slurred.

"I will... not..."

Sarandiel watched as a clear film covered his staticky anima, as if encasing him in resin. She let out a sigh as it flitted to the field, taking residence next to the others.

All this time they had one of the most important pieces to their puzzle sitting right in Cassus. She wondered why he hadn't been brought to her before or the fact that he was both an Alchemist and Monarch. Something didn't sit right with her. Once an anima became Wayward, it was set in stone. Not even Axton could bring them back from true death.

CHAPTER 8

SARANDIEL

Sarandiel sighed as she tended to a backlog of assignments. Axton had been busy with councils and she was eager to tell him what she learned on Cassus. Adding to her worry was the fact that they'd had sex. They'd had each other. It blew her mind. The evidence was clear in the soreness between her legs.

Desire had blinded her, and at the time, she wanted it. Yes, it was her idea. Yes, she wanted him so badly that she fucked the rules. But now she was freaking out about the repercussions of their actions. Her guilt was not about their intimacy. It was about the fear of getting caught and what that would mean. She could only blame herself if something were to happen to Axton.

Lost in her thoughts, she left her office and breezed down the empty hallway, most workers having gone to turn shifts with another set.

"Sarandiel."

She froze as she heard Michael's warm, syrupy voice. His feverish hand touched her bare elbow to turn her around. Subtly, she moved her arm from his grasp. She suddenly felt conscious of her short-sleeved blouse and shift skirt. Every part of her being recoiled at his touch.

"What is it?" Her stomach roiled at his closeness. *It's been over ten Sol cycles since you saw him last.* She reminded herself. He smirked, the air of cockiness wafting around him.

"It's been a while. Did you forget me already?" He stepped too close for comfort.

Michael was heart achingly handsome. Dark tan skin, green eyes, and wavy hair the color of richly tilled earth. He wore a dark brown tactical tee and black cargo pants. The emblem of the Celestial Legion covered his right pec with his General pin above it. Everything about him screamed warmth. Well, on the exterior. Inside, he was vile. She had experienced just how disgusting he could be, and she hated that he always knew where to find her.

"Of course. Why would I want to remember you?" Sarandiel's body shook as she withheld her pain and fury. She wasn't the meek Angel she used to be, but being around him made her feel small all over again.

"I'm far from forgettable. We were together for fifty-five Sol cycles. That's a lot of history to forget." Michael brushed one of her braids behind her shoulder, fingers gliding along her neck before he pulled away.

Sick, awful repulsion sat in her stomach like a stone. Her nose flared as she refused to back down.

"Oh right. How could I forget how you abused me when we were together? Who could ever want to forget that?" she hissed.

His eyes widened slightly, flaring bright emerald.

"I never laid a hand on you, Sara." His smirk grew, suddenly making him hideous.

How could she have ever thought him handsome? Love blindness would do a lot to cover it, that was for sure.

"*Don't* call me that. You didn't have to lay a hand on me to hurt me." She absentmindedly rubbed the scar on her wrist, her bracelets jingling softly.

Michael turned his gaze to her hands before looking back at her.

"You know, if you had just accepted me. Accepted the Claiming, we wouldn't be in this situation. If I didn't care, why would I bother coming back to seek you out? You look so much more beautiful up close."

Up close? What did that mean? She shook the thoughts away and glared at him.

"You should've just respected my decision. I said 'no' and you didn't like it. And thus, you *hurt* me. I am done with this conversation." She turned to leave, but he caught her elbow again.

"Michael, let me go."

"I'm sorry you took things that way. Can we at least talk about it?"

"That's not an apology, asshole, and I don't want to talk about it." Her shadows leapt from her to push him off. Michael's eyebrows drew tight in anger, and he opened his mouth to spew something at her before she felt a powerful presence not too far behind.

"And what exactly is going on here?" Axton's bass rumbled, barely contained fury in his tone. His accent thickened so much that there was a strong emphasis on the word 'here'.

Michael raised his gaze to Axton and took a step back.

"Just rehashing the past," he said slickly.

'Should I kill the wanker now or later?' Axton's voice traveled through her mind. She gave a small shake of her head as she kept her eyes on the Angel before her.

"It doesn't appear as if she wants to. Shouldn't you be assessing the Legion, General? If there is a rising threat, like everyone believes, my best Legionnaires need to be focused," Axton growled.

The Angel pursed his lips as he quickly glanced at Sarandiel before bowing and leaving, heading for the hall of portals.

Sarandiel sagged in relief. Axton steadied her with a hand on her elbow. She looked up at him, his blue flamed eyes lit with concern. She righted herself, smoothing her shirt, and clearing her throat.

"Fuck. I didn't mean to get caught alone with him."

"Shh, vixen, it is not your fault." Axton cupped her face before leaning in to kiss her.

"He always seems to catch me off guard, blindsiding me," she blurted before he could. Gah! Stupid! She snapped her mouth shut.

"Always? Does he do this often?" he snarled.

"Roughly every ten Sol cycles." She found it odd that he continued to harass her over the centuries.

"I'm going to end him." He took a step forward, but her body blocked him. Axton looked down at her in disbelief.

"You know you can't. What we did is illegal. How would you explain killing your General without reason? No one would believe my history with him. There's no proof, *remember*." She would be lying if she said she didn't wish to see Michael's head on a spike. But, as much of an asshole as he was, he was too important to the Legion.

"Fine. But that doesn't mean I cannot make his life bloody miserable." He rolled his eyes at her look of disapproval. "What?"

"You can't." She swatted his arm, shocked at his petulance.

"I'll be subtle. Make him work a few ceremonies. Put in some OT with the boots. Menial tasks." He gave her a wink and she rolled her eyes in exasperation.

"Well, now that you're here, I need to speak with you about what I found on Cassus." As they walked to his office, she told him the entirety of her visit. She could practically feel the frustration leaping off his body in waves.

"And no one thought to say a word about any of this?" he said, anger lacing his tone as he sat at his desk.

"Not a peep." She sighed as she sat in the chair across from him. "I've let the shadows listen, and there is definitely something up with Medius. You've been adamant about your Ascendents not failing, but if a group of mortal Alchemists can crack it, even a little, then it's something we have to raise alarms for. We need Tomis's Chaos Wielder." Axton's jaw clenched as frustration vibrated off him.

"No. We cannot, love. You know Deities are not to interfere with the happenings on Euhaven unless it is a risk to the entire realms."

"Aeshma was a risk to the realms before. What's to say she isn't now?" Sarandiel challenged.

"She does not have the same resources or support. Times have changed in the centuries since the Civil War. If she *were* to escape, it would not be easy for her," he said more calmly than she expected. "Sarandiel, a minute crack in an Ascendent we cannot find is worrisome, yes. But if we were to take the prophecy at face value, then now isn't the time. I don't fully trust it, but I also don't doubt it enough to use the Wielder. They are too powerful to use just for a potentiality. It would be a greater risk to use them earlier than they're supposed to." Axton shook his head, and she groaned in frustration.

"Will you at least have Gabriel assess Euhaven by using the Quasar Rangers? I have a feeling a Celestial is helping the Alchemists. It could only explain why they could make a crack in the Ascendent." She yawned before standing, and stretched. "A small contingent of Rangers, perhaps Demies, can find out. And maybe find the location as well."

"That is a brilliant idea. I will talk with Gabriel and have him set up a reconnaissance mission." He mimicked Sarandiel by rising to his feet and coming around the desk. Axton leaned in close, making her heart skip a beat. He took a deep breath. "Can I come by tonight?" he murmured.

"About that..." Sarandiel looked away from his confused expression. "I think I acted too hastily." It hurt to say it. To admit that she may have made a mistake, even though it didn't feel like it in her heart.

"We can make this work." He turned her chin up to look at him.

"No. We could be arrested, or even killed. You are too important to this realm. The risk is too great." She sighed, stepping back and trying to ignore the ache in her belly. Why didn't she think more about this the night before?

"You realize you are important too? Not just to me, but to the realm as well. They see you for what you truly are; an amazing Angel who cares for them and the animas deeply. I am drawn to you in ways I've never felt before. Is it a risk? Yes. But I will fight for us. I would do anything, even go up against the Concilium, if it meant being with you."

His words left her momentarily speechless. He always had a way of doing that. Axton stepped forward, taking her elbows gently and pulling her in.

"I feel the same way. It's magnetic, I know," she breathed as his hands glided up her arms. Her body shuddered under his touch as those fingers traced her collar bone and ended at her jaw. Using his thumb under her chin, he tilted her head up.

"Magnetic is an understatement, Sarandiel," he growled before giving her a mind-blowing kiss. Slick gathered between her legs, making her moan into his mouth. If she didn't stop this now, she wouldn't be able to turn back. And if she didn't turn back...

"Wait..." she gasped as she pulled away. He took a step away, honoring her space, looking as flustered as she felt. "I want this, I do. But you're important to me too. I couldn't bear to see you at risk or hurt because of me." She put her hand out in between them, as if to shake his hand. "We can't do this. I would never forgive myself if anything were to happen to you." Her hand shook as the emotions tightened her chest. "I think it's best we remain cordial. Friends."

Sarandiel bit her lip. His eyes honed in to them before looking down at her hand. She felt like she was giving him whiplash, and guilt ate at her, the look in his eyes making her feel worse. He probably thought she only wanted a one-night stand. The thought twisted her gut.

"If that is what you wish."

Sad. He sounded so sad. Fuck. She wanted to take it back but she couldn't. When she nodded, he took her hand and gave it a shake.

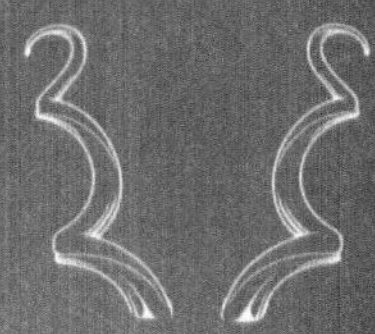

CHAPTER 9

AXTON

The smell of sulfur assaulted Axton's nose as he phased into Mordax, hovering in the air. The sprawling city was dark under the crimson sky. In the distance a smoking volcano rumbled, nearing its weekly eruption. Large, ice blue leather wings propelled him forward as he flew through the city blocks, eyeing the people on the sidewalks.

Those who lived in Mordax loved the dark. And while dark they were, evil they were not. They all had a role to play in managing the various forms of punishment Axton assigned. Warehouses and buildings were set up for different types of sentences and torture. The animas here suffered the crimes they committed or worse.

Ahead was the Tenura. It was a prison for the worst animas. As the Deity of Death, he visited weekly to assess each red alert anima. Some he even took great pleasure in punishing.

His combat boots thundered as he landed before the large, circular, domed building. Though the walls appeared crumbling and desolate, it was a façade for the truth. Inside was the worst place to be in Mordax.

The sounds of wailing reverberated around him as he entered the prison. He turned to the Demon at the entrance, who held a holoport in hand. Yellow eyes turned up to Axton, and the Demon blanched, orange skin paling.

"What floor is he on?" Axton's voice was a disembodied growl as he spoke through the skull shaped helm covering his head and face. His black horns escaped through the helm and almost reaching the ceiling, tipped in crimson.

♪♪ "Lightning Over Mexico" by Tom Morello, The Bloody Beetroots, Ana Tijoux

"T-ten, my Lord," the Demon stuttered, bowing so low his red, curling, ram-like horns practically touched the floor.

"Get up," he said with an eye roll.

The Demon righted himself as Axton walked past and made his way up, floor by floor. The spiral staircase smelled repugnant, the damp seeping through every other odor. Cells circled a watchtower and punishment platform for animas that needed public humiliation. The screams of an anima currently on the whipping post echoed throughout the prison. As he entered the tenth floor, the animas started wailing. Skin blackened, their bodies were broken down, and flesh dripped from their bones. They were stuck in a perpetual state of rot.

Axton's steps rang out as he made his way down the hall of cells to one of the most recent red alert animas. The black cape attached to his shoulder guards billowed around him as he came to a halt in front of the cell. Slowly opening the door, he watched as the male before him attempted to free himself from the large tree root impaling him to the wall.

Axton imagined he looked like the physical embodiment of punishment with his arms covered in split, grotesque Deity symbols, skin the sallowness of death, and thick claws that clicked against the bars of the cell door.

"Your Wielding will not work here Bethnal," Axton rumbled through his helm. The Earth Wielder diverted his gaze, shuddering at Axton's closeness. "Do you understand why it is you are here, Bethnal?"

"Yes..." he whimpered, skin dripping from his face. Axton flexed his hands, gauntlets clinking, as he took a step forward.

Bethnal shrieked in fear, turning his face to keep from being touched.

"And why is it you are here, Earth Wielder?" he snarled, grasping Bethnal's sickly jaw and turned him to meet his flaming blue eyes that shone through the helm.

The anima shook his head, blood dripping from his eyes and ears. Axton gripped his chin tighter, the skin sloughing off and exposing bone. The male cried out as his body shook.

"Answer me!"

"I killed my sons," he sobbed. "I killed my boys, and I don't know why." Axton let him go, taking a step back.

"Why don't you know?" he said, leaning on the tree root and making anima yell. "This pain you're feeling, your sons felt much worse." Anger overcame him as it did when he doled out a punishment.

"I..." he coughed, blood dripping from his mouth. "I lost control. My wife found out I was having an affair. A disgusting fool I am." He thrashed his head in agony. Suddenly he snarled, gnashing his teeth. "No! They fucking deserved it! She shouldn't have argued with me. So, I fucked someone else." The sudden change of demeanor concerned Axton.

"Your sons deserved to die because you were upset. Is that correct?" he said, voice dark as he dragged the root, making the anima scream. Bethnal sobbed, coming out of his anger.

"No, no, they didn't. I don't know why I did it. I would never have cheated on my wife, but I was so angry and I wanted revenge." Bloody tears dripped from his lidless eyes. "I didn't..." Thrashing his head, he howled, "They *deserved* it! They shouldn't have fucking got in my way. Fucking bastards!"

"Again, why are you here?" Axton growled.

"Because I killed my sons."

"Why else?"

"Because I fucking enjoyed it!" His laugh was sinister and felt wrong. The anima before him was broken. Axton had seen his fair share of broken animas but nothing of this nature. Bethnal sobbed again. "It was a wave. It overcame me and the others."

"The others?" he asked, shoving the root deeper into the wall, widening the hole in the male's torso.

"The other Wielders! The ones that were with me at the bar." Fuck, this couldn't be happening. "One minute we were talking shit about our wives and the next we were finding the next woman to fuck." Bethnal shook his head, evil smile pulling his mouth despite the lack of lips. "It felt so fucking good. So good to get my dick wet by someone other than that bitch!"

"Where were you when this happened?"

"Melhold." The anima wailed, "Are my boys in Pax? My wife?" Blood poured from his mouth, making him choke.

"Tell me why you killed them?"

"I don't know!"

"Lies. Tell me why you killed them? I will not repeat myself again." Axton knew the answer was going to be one he didn't want to hear. Especially as the anima let out a manic laugh.

"Wrath! Wrath!" The anima choked again on his own blood. "Wrath!" He repeated like a mantra. Axton stuck his hand into the male's mouth before jerking it down to rip his jaw off. His tongue hung limply as he cried, moaning in pain. Bethnal's pleading eyes bore into his.

"You do not deserve to know because of the things you have done." Axton held the bloodied tongue. "But your sons would want you to know. They forgave you because they knew you were not yourself." He pulled slowly, the anima's eyes bulging. "Your wife survived. Your boys have moved on to Pax."

Bloodied tears fell from Bethnal's eyes, relief slumping his body as much as it could around the tree root. Axton wrapped his hand around the tongue, pulling it out of the male.

"Do not think this gives you solace. You will relive seeing them die over and over until you are ready for Cassus."

The smell of the male's agony was savory and satiated his hunger for violence. Axton chuckled as he dropped the tongue on the floor.

"I will see you next week."

CHAPTER 10
SARANDIEL

Over the course of the next month, Axton spent more time with Sarandiel after his hard assignments. They often met at Hollows or his office with the door open at her request. She could feel the strain between them as they attempted friendship. As much as they tried to avoid it, they couldn't help flirting with each other. It left an ache, having had him and needing to deny it all over again.

"No wait. The intern has a crush on you?" she laughed before stuffing her face with spicy brown noodles.

The two of them were sitting on the office floor, assignments spread out between them as they ate South Asherite food. Medius had some amazing dishes. Too bad Celestials couldn't manifest food, otherwise she'd eat her fill of spicy noodles. Apparently, the atoms got all jacked up when they tried.

"Why am I not surprised?"

"They're always like that." Axton shrugged, grabbing soft bread to dip into his curry.

He looked so relaxed, leaning against the obsidian desk, the top few buttons of his white shirt undone. The sleeves were rolled up to his elbows, veins along his hands and forearms flexing with each movement. It was rare to see the Deity so comfortable.

"Sarandiel?"

She blinked several times, having not realized that she was staring.

"Sorry?" She quickly took a bite of food to cover her ass.

Axton gave her a knowing grin but let her off the hook.

"Tell me, where do you see yourself in the next five centuries?" he asked as he ruffled his hair, a few strands falling over his forehead.

Her pulse sped at the view.

She internally scolded herself before answering, "I'd like to see myself working with the children on Pax." She smiled at the thought.

"Really? Like what?" he asked, genuine interest in his expression.

"Well, with the influx of deaths came an alarming number of animas of children. We have parks on Pax, but we could use more. They take quite a bit of time to construct because of Pax's rotation. The children deserve a space to explore without the overwhelm of so many other animas." She took a bite of her food as she mused, "I've enjoyed working with the children when I visit Pax."

"You visit Pax? How often?" Axton asked with raised eyebrows. "Pax does not need much managing, though I go once a month. How have I never seen you there?"

"I don't stay within the facility. I explore the cities and the parks—obviously. It's a pleasure speaking with the animas. They're comfortable, but they enjoy the follow-ups. Children are children," she laughed before sighing sadly. "Many are there without their biological parents, and while the adult animas take them in, they need more space."

"I admit, I am quite embarrassed that I have never considered that before," Axton said, rubbing his smooth jaw. "I think it's a brilliant idea, and that we should get on it as soon as possible."

Her mouth dropped in surprise.

"What? But—"

"I know we have concerns with Medius. But that does not mean we cannot get started. When you have the time, bring me a proposal, and we will go from there." The smile he gave her made her stomach do a flip. The respect that shone in his eyes had her heart fluttering again.

"Your support means a lot to me, Ax." *What did I just call him? Fuck, it was so inappropriate!*

"Ax?" he said with eyebrows raised. Something must have telegraphed on her face because he said, "It's quite all right, love. I'm rather fond of it."

Axton smirked as he reached for his food. Sarandiel watched as he ate, the way the soaked bread passed through his lips and his navy tongue licking the sauce afterward.

He raised an eyebrow, grin slowly turning up his mouth. Ah fuck. He caught her. "Would you like to have a taste?" he murmured, voice dipping low.

Honestly, she did, but not in the way he meant.

"Nope. That's ok." She could feel herself flushing.

He leaned over, holding the bread.

"It's very good, trust me."

The look in his eyes tightened her core. They shouldn't be doing this. Before she thought it through, she nodded.

"Ok sure," she said before leaning in and opening her mouth.

Axton slowly ran the wet bread across her lower lip, spreading the sauce. She took a bite, lightly grazing her teeth on the tips of his fingers, making him groan softly. What was she *doing*? Closing her eyes, she savored the taste of the curry, licking her lips slowly. Spices exploded in her mouth, the taste of ginger and cardamom most prevalent. Indeed, it was very good.

"Would you like more, vixen?" His tone made her snap her eyes open.

It'd been a while since he called her that. He was closer now and she could feel her nipples hardening. Fuck. She wanted more. So much more.

"Axton, you're going to ruin me..." she whispered. Her eyes flicked to the open door which suddenly shut with a snap of his fingers.

"Tell me to stop and I will."

She knew he respected her enough to honor her request if she asked.

"I'm at war with myself," she confessed. "I want this. I want us." She shivered as he cupped her face. His hand felt so good on her skin. "But what if we're caught? What happens then?"

"I'm the fucking Deity of Death. Do you honestly think I'd let them take you? I already told you I'd face them, go *through* them if I have to."

"But…" Sarandiel leaned into his hand, scooting close enough to feel his warmth. Licking her lips, she knew her answer.*

"Fuck them…" he growled as he pulled her into a passionate kiss, groaning when she opened for him.

Their tongues clashed, the kiss hot and heavy. She bit his lower lip before sucking it in. Axton gripped the back of her neck as he pulled her to straddle his lap. She moaned as she ground on his erection. He tilted her head back so he could plunge into her mouth deeply, his tongue wrapping around hers.

It felt right. It felt good. How did she last a month without touching him? Without kissing him?

"I need you. I can't deny it anymore," she breathed against his lips.

He nipped at her chin, trailing his way to her neck.

"Love, you're all I've thought about," he said in between bites and kisses. "In meetings, during assignments." Gripping her ass he murmured, "When I had nothing but my hand to satisfy the craving for your sweet pussy." Her back arched, brushing her aching nipples against his chest through their shirts. "It's not the same."

"Axton…" she purred as he gripped her tighter.

"Say my name again, vixen." His growl vibrated through her, shooting straight to her pulsing core.

"Axton." The feel of his long tongue licking a line from her neck to between her breasts made her whimper.

"We're going. I need to hear you scream my name."

She panted as he stood up with her legs around his waist and phased them to the living room of his penthouse. Axton sat her on the bar that separated the living room from the kitchen, putting her at face level with him. He gripped her hips as he pulled her close, kissing her until she saw stars. Liquid heat poured between her thighs.

"Sarandiel, you are perfection. I could look at you all day." He pulled her shirt over her head. "Did you think about me? Did you fuck yourself with your fingers, wishing they were mine?" He cupped her breasts, thumbs running over her nipples through her lace bra.

___

♪♪ "Close" by Nick Jonas, Tove Lo

"Yes. I couldn't get you off my mind." Her hips jerked as he snapped her bra off, tossing it over his shoulder. Gripping his shirt, she cried out as he widened his jaw to take her whole breast in his mouth. "Oh fuck!"

His tongue flicked her nipple, his hand sliding down her stomach and into her pants. He groaned as his fingers found her dripping core.

'Already so wet for me.' The Deity's voice caressed her mind. Agile fingers rubbed her clit in circular motions while teeth prickled around the flesh of her breast.

"Shit, Ax, that feels so good." She rocked her hips, grinding on his hand. Sarandiel yelped in surprise as two of his fingers extended and thickened before entering her pussy. "Oh! I did *not* know you could do that."

'I am a Deity of many surprises.' His tone was one of peak masculinity.

Her eyes rolled as he drove his fingers in her, thumb rubbing her clit. She clenched around him, whimpering.

"I'm going to come!"

Axton tightened his mouth over her breast, adding a flicker of pain while he fucked her until her orgasm crashed through her. Pulling away from her, he lifted her long enough to pull her jeans and underwear off before consuming her sensitive cunt. Sarandiel grabbed his delicate horns, the Deity symbols lighting up as she ground against him. She stroked them, making him hum delightfully against her.

"Do you like that, my devastation?"

Her back arched as he gripped her ass and wrapped her legs around his neck. He thrust his tongue into her in response. Shadows erupted around them as her body trembled with pleasure. They made quick work of tearing away his clothes. He groaned as they stroked his cock, the sensation sending waves of pleasure down her spine.

'Naughty angel.' Growling, Axton stood straight, holding her on his shoulders while Sarandiel continued to fuck his mouth. He pushed her against the wall, pumping his tongue into her. His teeth

nicked her clit with a slight edge of pain, making her jerk against him. A second orgasm built in her core, and she tightened her thighs around his face. *'Tighter. Suffocate me.'*

Using his horns, she pulled herself as close as she could get, locking her knees behind his head. Roughly, she rode him with his tongue writhing in her with the same intensity.

"Axton!" she screamed as her orgasm barreled down.

Sloppy sounds of his mouth on her gushing cunt filled her ears. While loosening her hold, Axton's tongue slid out of her, and he helped her to stand. Fuck, his face was glistening from the force of her orgasm, the juices dripping from his chin.

"Hmmm. You taste so sweet," he rumbled through his extended jaw. He wrapped his tongue around his wet clawed fingers he'd fucked her with and sucked them clean.

"Claws…" Sarandiel breathed, taking his hand and running her tongue up one.

"Fuck, vixen." His cock jerked, and she suddenly needed to taste him.

"Sit," she commanded, nodding to the nearby ottoman.

"So needy." Axton chuckled as he sat.

She settled herself between his legs, his cock jutting out. It was a wonderful shade of ice blue, darkening at the head. He was so big that she was sure she wouldn't be able to take him completely in her mouth. But she didn't care. She wanted it all. His sapphire eyes flared brightly as he watched her soft lips part around his dick.

Gripping his shaft, she stroked him as she bobbed. First paying special attention to the dark blue tip of the head, and then sucking him in as far as she could. He inhaled sharply when she glided her teeth across the soft, velvet flesh.

"Hmmm," he purred. "You're amazing at sucking my dick." The praise had her pussy dripping and encouraged her to take as much of him in as she could.

Grabbing her braids, he thrust into her mouth, making her gag. Saliva dripped down her chin as she relaxed her throat.

"Fuck, you look so beautiful taking my dick."

She whimpered as he pumped into her. Her shadows pinched

his nipples, tugging on the piercings, making him hiss.

"Be a good angel and make me come," he groaned.

Axton fucked her mouth as deeply as he could, and she took all he had to give, sucking harder and stroking faster. With a roar, Axton unloaded his come in her mouth, pouring over her breasts. The effects of his arousal had her body singing, feeling as if it were floating. Desire flooded her, making her more aroused than she thought possible.

Sarandiel sat back on her heels, rubbing the hot cerulean fluid over dark brown breasts and nipples before licking her fingers. "So delicious." She winked as his cock remained hard.

She squealed when he lifted her as he stood, wrapping her legs around him and thrusting in her soaking pussy.

"Oh, Creator… Shit!" Moaning, she gyrated her hips against his. His hands dug into her hair, tilting her head back to expose her neck to him.

"The only name you should be screaming is *mine*." Axton drove into her, hitting her cervix and making her cry out.

"Axton! Keep doing that!" She gasped when he repeated, her legs twitching from the jolt of pain and pleasure.

Pushing her against the wall, his tongue snaked out to bind her wrists above her head. Gripping her ass, he hiked her up, hooking his elbows under her knees. It allowed him to fuck her so deep she swore she could feel him in her stomach.

'Your cunt fits my dick perfectly.' The Deity moaned as her shadows massaged his balls and slid between his ass cheeks to stroke his asshole. *'Angel, you know exactly what to do in order to please me. I'm going to devastate you.'* Axton thrusted deep, driving in and out of her.

"Oh fuck! Axton." Tears of pleasure leaked from her eyes as his claws dug into her ass.

She sobbed wildly, her deliciously sore cunt overflowing on his cock. Claws lightly pierced her skin, making her writhe. She wasn't one for pain, but Axton knew how to take it to the perfect edge. Her shadows swirled, making him groan as they latched to his nipple piercings.

'This delicious pussy is so hungry for my dick.' The words had her whimpering as she felt her orgasm nearing. She whined at not being able to touch him, her hands bound against the wall. *'Cry out my name, vixen.'*

"Axton!" she screamed as he fucked her deeply.

'That's it. Such a good angel. Come for me.' Legs shaking, the massive orgasm overcame her. The room shook with the power of her pleasure, her arousal flowing over his thighs. *'Take this come, vixen. Take it all.'* He growled before filling her.

Their combined fluids poured down his legs to the floor. Body twitching, Axton let her wrists go, licking at the flesh gently to soothe her aches. Her body shook as he let her legs down. He wrapped her in his arms, helping to ease the tremors.

"I don't think we can just be friends," she huffed against his chest. His rumbling chuckle vibrated against her cheek.

"No, vixen. I don't suppose we can either."

CHAPTER 11

SARANDIEL

"**Y**ou do not have to stay if you don't wish it," Axton told Sarandiel the next day.

They were in the conference room, readying for a meeting with the Demon Council from Medius. They were meant to lay low, monitor things, and report to Axton anything of importance. That they hadn't told him about the rise of wrathful deaths put the Deity in a sour mood.

"Yes, it's all right." Sarandiel chuckled. "Do you know how many of these I've sat for? Where would you be without my notes and impeccable memory?"

"Very true." Axton grinned and it lit up the room. He didn't smile often, and it was a sight to behold. He nodded to the stool next to him, near the head of the table. "Sit next to me."

"Already planned to." She winked as she sat. Oh, she had plenty of things planned.

His smile dropped when the Demons entered the conference room. His brows drew together, letting them all know he was furious. There was a Demon for each country of Euhaven.

"My Lord Axton," came the tenor of Norrix Aimes. Sarandiel bit back a groan.

The head of the Demon Council rubbed her the wrong way. Red and black encased every part of his body. From the black three-piece suit with red pinstripes, to his stark red hair and eyes. His pale skin was almost translucent under the lights. He was a pissant and a suck up. How much red did one person need?

"Do not 'my Lord' me, Norrix. Sit over there." Axton sneered at the Demon.

Norrix moved to his assigned spot in silence. Sarandiel opened her holoport while Axton leaned back in his chair, crossing one foot onto the opposite knee. Watching from under her lashes, she admired the way his white button up moved over his muscular chest and how his powerful legs fit into his dark grey slacks. She took a gulp of her water, feeling his eyes on her before he turned them to the Demons.

"Tomis has approached me about a rise in wrathful fueled deaths in Medius." His voice rumbled through the room. "Why am I just hearing about this from her when *you all* should have informed me first?"

"Euhaven is Euhaven. We didn't think anything different from the norm." Edam spoke from the end of the table. The Demon looked unsure, his golden-brown eyes flittering about. His tan skin was flushed, sweat covering his brow.

He is lying, she thought.

"We would've informed you if we truly thought things were amiss," Norrix said smoothly. Edam nodded quickly, the other six Demons remaining quiet.

Axton grabbed one binder from the pile next to him and slammed onto the table, making everyone jump.

"These are from Melhold alone."

He grabbed another and dropped it on top of the first. "Silvermoon."

He picked up two more. "Alburg and Calñar." Axton growled, the table vibrating from the force. "These are your domains." He pointed at Edam and Norrix. Edam paled while Norrix smirked.

"These cities are all known for their riotous behavior. It's hardly cause for concern. I assure you I have been monitoring the state of the cities as ordered." The Demon was testing his luck. Even Sarandiel knew it. "Potroya hasn't seen any increased deaths. Neither has South Asherai, Shayce, and Gailux. There isn't a rise on a global scale. So, I don't think it's anything other than the norm for those cities." He nodded his chin to the six Demon representatives.

She watched as Axton processed the information.

He leaned forward to rest his elbows on the table. "Fine. Then I want you all to update me on the remaining statuses of your domains."

"Lord Axton, may I ask you a question before we begin updates?" Norrix piped up again.

It was clear the Deity was fighting a retort but gave a nod instead.

"Go ahead, Norrix."

"Are we any closer to a decision on whether Demons can return to the general public on Euhaven? Living in the dark is not as appealing to some as the others. Not all of us can return to Orcus." There was genuine concern on the Demon's face.

"No, there isn't. As you've all heard, there's a threat against Medius. If that threat were to come to pass, then chaos will descend on the realm. We can't add one more log to the fire." Axton looked at each of them as he spoke.

"But Angels are allowed," Norrix huffed. "They're publicly living while we have to hide. We are more than just 'logs' to a fire. We are a people. A people *you* created."

"Angels are not publicly living, and if they are, then I will inform the Quasars to find them and bring them to the Tenura."

"Angels and Demies have been hiding in plain sight for centuries. Ever since Melvina sacrificed herself, there hasn't been a Deity with proper domain over Medius. *Demons* are the ones obeying your command." Norrix clenched his jaw when Axton leveled a glare at him.

"If this is true, then why am I just bloody hearing about it? I am not all knowing. How do you expect me to make decisions if I do not know the full scope?"

And round they went back to the original topic. Everything seemed to be falling through the cracks, and she knew it had to frustrate the Deity since he relied on order and consistency.

"I will look into it further."

"All right." Norrix begrudgingly accepted the answer.

"Now. Please proceed with any other updates."

The next hour droned on as each Demon gave updates.

The topic took a turn to politics around the election of new Council heads, and Axton looked visibly disinterested while they bickered amongst themselves. Elections were Demon business.

Sarandiel tried to hide her devious smirk as she let a shadow loose to snake around Axton's ankle. The briefest widening of his eyes was the only sign that he noticed. She continued to take notes as she willed the shadows to travel along the inside of his slacks, writhing along the skin of his strong thighs. Extensions of herself, each of her shadows' caress tingled in her palms. Muscles rippled under her shadowy touch, making her clench her thighs together. The shadows made it to his cock and wrapped around it to stroke him.

Axton coughed, grabbing his water and giving her a side eye. Sarandiel smiled innocently as she looked at her holoport and back with a shrug.

'*What are you doing, vixen?*' His words fluttered through her mind sensually. Her shadows continued to stroke him while she made others flow up his shirt to play with his pierced nipples. '*Fuck…*' He growled in her mind.

Outwardly, no one would know what she was doing, or that he was affected. Sarandiel pumped his cock, the length rock hard under her shadowy touch. '*You understand I'm going to punish you for this?*'

She could feel herself getting slick, trying to dial back her arousal or else everyone would know.

"Fine, fine. I've heard enough." Axton cleared his throat as she continued to stroke him. She nearly giggled when he took another large swig of his water. "Monitor these deaths, and for any sudden spikes in crime. You're dismissed."

After the Demons filed out, Axton turned his ardent gaze on her.

"Such a naughty angel." He groaned as she increased the pressure around his cock.

"Who? Me?" Sarandiel said salaciously. "I don't know what you're talking about." She finished her notes and closed her holoport. A group of assistants made their way into the room, diverting their eyes from the Deity of War.

"We need to discuss the notes you took today. My office. Now," he said through gritted teeth. She brought the shadows back to her with a smirk.

"All right," she murmured as she brushed by him. His grunt gave her the best satisfaction.

Sarandiel took her sweet time walking next to him. Delaying to say hi to another worker, stopping to check the mail. By the time they were in his office, he had snapped the door shut, locked it, and pulled her into a world-shattering kiss. He tangled his hand in her braids, gripping tightly. She moaned into his mouth as their tongues clashed and rubbed together. His free hand grabbed her ass, grinding her against his hard erection.

"I should serve your punishment right here, right now." Axton growled as he kissed her neck, suckling on it before grazing his teeth on the soft flesh.*

She gasped as he tilted her head back and extended his navy tongue to dip into the opening of her blouse. It snaked into her bra and coiled around her nipple, making her moan. He moved his hand from her ass to her mouth, quieting her. Axton drew his tongue back before nipping at her neck.

"Shh. No one can hear us," he breathed.

Fuck, he was right. What they were doing was forbidden. She should've stopped it, but his tongue found its way back into her bra and her brain short circuited. She gasped softly against his hand, shadows escaping her to push their way into his slacks, circling his cock. He groaned against her as his hips jerked.

"Shh," Sarandiel whispered against his hand.

'*Vixen.*'

"Devastation."

Axton growled quietly, the vibration shooting straight to her core. He pulled away from her to push her shirt and bra up. He widened his jaw to take her entire breast into his mouth. She fought back a pleasurable yelp as his tongue flicked her nipple and his teeth bit the flesh.

"Fuck, Ax," she whimpered.

♪ "Sweat" by ZAYN

'Hmm, I love that,' he said in response to the nickname. *'Free my dick.'* His voice glided along her mind like a caress, making her eyes roll.

Sarandiel pulled him out, gripping his large girth. Using both hands, she stroked him, making him moan around her breast.

'You stroke me so well.' The praise had her pussy flooding with arousal. Axton moved to her other breast, her nipple aching for friction.

"Your tongue. Holy Creator!" Sarandiel sucked in his thumb, biting down to keep from moaning too loudly.

Moving his hand from her braids, he pushed up her skirt and slid his hand into her soaking underwear.

'Fuck, you're so wet for me.'

Sarandiel whimpered as he thrust two of his fingers into her. Her strokes around his cock increased in time with his thrusting into her cunt. She needed him in her.

"Please. I need you in me," she whined, feeling herself close to the edge.

Axton chuckled as he pulled away, sliding his hand out of her. He swirled his tongue around his fingers, humming at the taste of her juices.

"Get on your knees, love." His tone darkened.

Sarandiel dropped to her knees without hesitation, licking her lips at the sight of his cock. The azure tip glistened and she leaned in for a taste. Axton swatted at her when she reached for him.

"No. Hands in your lap. You will watch as I pleasure myself." He groaned before he spit on his length and stroked slowly.

Rubbing her thighs together, she ached for friction. She looked up to find him gazing at her. His eyes were lit brightly with blue flame, his black horns looming above. Silver Deity symbols glowed brightly. Fuck, he was so sexy.

"That's a beautiful sight. Watching you on your knees and following directions." Axton bit his lip.

Every praise he gave her made her wetter. It made her desire increase to a new level. Catching a bead of moisture at the tip of his dick, Axton ran his finger across her lips, wetting them with his arousal. Sarandiel whimpered as she licked and tasted him.

"I know you want more, love." His eyes blazed as his strokes increased and a growl left his throat. "Right now, I'm going to come." He kept his fiery gaze on her. "Are you ready? Are you ready for my come?" he growled.

She hummed her consent, nodding as she looked up at him. "Yes," she breathed.

"Good. You're such a good angel."

Fuck! Her pussy throbbed.

Axton's hips jerked forward as he thrusted against his hand. "F-fuck I'm coming, vixen. Open your mouth." He bit his hand, and a strangled cry left his lips as he pumped himself once more before coming.

Cerulean come shot out in jets, filling her mouth quicker than she could swallow. It overflowed, running down her chin, neck, and onto her white blouse, staining it a shade of dark blue. It tingled across her body, sending waves of pleasure to her core. She could feel herself getting high off the taste. He pulled out and knelt before her to kiss her deeply, licking his own cum from her mouth.

"I need more," Sarandiel begged.

Axton smirked, a mischievous glint in his eyes.

"I know, but that's too bad..." he whispered against her mouth.

What the fuck?

"Serves you right for teasing me in public."

"No! Please, I'm sorry," she whined.

Axton returned to cleaning her up, humming as he did so. Sarandiel moaned softly as he licked her breasts, purposely avoiding her nipples. He sat back on his heels, waving a hand and replacing her blouse with a clean one.

"Be a good angel and I'll reward you later."

She narrowed her eyes at him. Devastation indeed.

By that evening, Sarandiel's body was thrumming with need. Axton had flirted with her, touching her when no one was looking. He repaid her every tease and left her wanting more. It was the wildest foreplay she ever had.

'Meet me in the garage, vixen.' Came the sooth caress of Axton's voice in her mind. It sent pleasure straight to her core.

How could this Deity's voice alone make her so wet?

She straightened her office before grabbing her belongings. Stepping into the cool air of the garage, she took a big inhale and exhaled slowly. Wondering why she was here, she turned to the purr of an engine to her right. The large space was empty save for the beauty in front of her.

"Since when do Deities drive? You can phase or fly wherever you want." Sarandiel snorted, walking toward the sleek monochromatic sports hovercar.

The hood curved gracefully, the hovercar was narrower in the front and wider at the back. The windows were so tinted that it was impossible to see inside. She had to admit, it was a fine specimen of technological ingenuity. It hovered a foot above the road, Axton leaning on the door, legs crossed at the ankles and his hands in his pockets. The smile on his face made her heart flutter. He had the most wonderful smile.

"These are one of my favorite inventions from Medius." He patted the hood as if the car were a pet. "It's a different high than what we get when flying. They're fast, dangerous, and thrilling." The passenger side door lifted toward the sky. "Get in and I'll show you."

The heat in his words implied enough. She quickly looked around before hopping into the car. As the door closed, the smell of leather and frost filled her nose. It was plush, the dashboard lit with different screens, none of which she understood except the GPS.

"Well, isn't this fancy." Sarandiel chuckled as Axton slid into the car, his slacks whispering along the seat.

His presence ate up all the air and she could feel her pulse quicken. They slid on their seatbelts before he pressed some buttons on the dash to get them moving. He looked at ease with one wrist resting on the steering wheel, sleeves rolled up to his elbows.

"Here we go," he murmured as he suddenly accelerated.

"I'll admit. I've never been in one of these, which is saying something. I should've when they were first invented," she said as she watched the buildings blur outside.

The roads were empty, which made for smooth driving. Holy shit, they were going fast. Yelping, she grabbed his hand as they took a sharp turn. He grinned as he moved his hand to her thigh, gripping it with reassurance.

"Relax. I know what I'm doing, love."

Oh, she knew that already. The feel of his hand so close to the hem of her skirt made her want to squirm. Axton was right, the adrenaline was different from flying. It convinced her that she had to learn to drive herself so that she could experience this rush whenever she wanted. Her heart sped as his hands slowly moved up, escaping under her skirt.

"What are you doing, Ax?" she breathed.

His dark grin had her shifting in her seat. Heat shot to her core, pulsing as his hand climbed higher.

"I can smell how wet you are for me." His growl circled the tight quarters of the car.

Sarandiel arched her back, opening her legs slowly.

Keeping his eyes on the road, his fingers found her dripping pussy. "Fuck, no panties? Naughty angel."

"I tossed them. They were too wet," she moaned. Fingers found her clit, making her buck. "Oh fuck..." she whimpered. She was so sensitive that she was sure she'd climax within minutes.

"Well, that earned you a reward," he purred, voice dropping to a sexy octave.

All it took was three strokes and she was coming. She grabbed his forearm as she rocked her hips. Sarandiel cried out as he thrust into her, fingers thickening into blunted claws. Axton took another sharp turn, accelerating as they hit the expressway. The rush from the fast car and his claws in her cunt sent another orgasm through her.

"Creator above!" she cried out. Her body fell limp against the seat as she panted.

Axton chuckled as he pulled his claws from her to lick. "So fucking sweet." *

Taking a sharp turn off an exit, the car swerved before he pulled into an empty parking lot. He threw the car into park and growled, "Get over here."

She scrambled into his lap, maneuvering not so gracefully over the gear shift and bumping against the steering wheel, beeping the car horn in the process. They chuckled as he put the back of his seat down.

"Vixen, I need to be in you," he breathed as she worked to undo his belt and slacks. She kissed him deeply, his tongue thrusting into her mouth.

"I need you in me too," Sarandiel panted desperately as she pulled his cock out. She cried out as he gripped her hips and slammed her on him, cock filling her to the hilt. "Axton!" she moaned as he bucked his hips while she rode him.

"Fuck me," he moaned deeply, claws now digging into her ass. She ground harder, their fucking a frenzy. One claw played at the puckering of her asshole, making her jolt. "Does my vixen like that?" She whined in response before his navy tongue snaked around her throat.

"Tighter," she whispered before he did as she asked.

Her pussy flooded over his cock, her hands gripping his shirt as the pleasure filled her up. Claws dug into her ass, causing a prickling of pain that had her mewling indulgently. Just as her vision started to blur, he released his hold around her neck. Euphoria filled her as she took a long gasp of air.

Stunning. Absolutely stunning, my vixen. His voice caressed her mind as his hips thrust upward, cock as deep as it could go. *You look beautiful bouncing on my dick.* Her eyes rolled as he tightened the hold around her neck again. *Eyes on me, angel.*

♪ "I Want To" by Rosenfeld

Snapping her eyes open, she met his sapphire gaze. Seeing his tongue extending around her neck had her rocking against him faster. Another orgasm was riding up her spine.

"Axton," she breathed through the hold. Using his tongue like a leash, he pulled her closer to him to wrap his jaws around her throat. His teeth glided across the flesh, making her shudder and her pace increase. If he were a different type of Deity, he could easily tear her throat out. The fear of the thought shot more pleasure down to her aching cunt.

'Love, you're drowning me in your arousal. You know how to fuck me just the way I like it.' He moaned in her mind. The hold on her ass tightened on the edge of pain as he encouraged her to move faster and grind himself deeper into her pussy. *'Come on my dick, vixen. Be a good angel for me.'*

A mind-blowing orgasm crashed through her as he loosened his tongue around her neck. The car shook as he pulled his tongue away from her to roar his pleasure and filled her as much as she could take. Their shared arousal doused his lap and the seat under them.

"Shit, you devastate me every time." Sarandiel chuckled, body twitching with aftershocks of her orgasm.

Axton hummed in agreement as he nuzzled her cheek, tongue licking her neck and soothing the aches. She closed her eyes to the sensation as his claws turned back to normal and his hands massaged her ass.

"You do something to me," she whispered, leaning into his touch and nuzzling his face before their noses touched. He drew his tongue back to him, righting his jaw.

"Same, vixen. You do something to me too," he said softly before kissing her.

Whatever it was, she knew she wouldn't be the same again, that life without Axton was no longer possible. He pulled her close, resting her head on his shoulder.

"Don't let go," she said softly.

"No, love. Never."

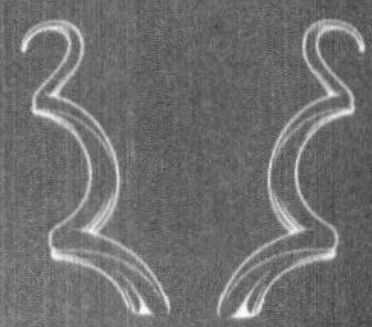

CHAPTER 12

AXTON

The sounds of grunts, bullets, and more, echoed around him as Axton walked toward the Celestial Legion training field. Across the vast greenery, Legionnaires were training in various units, overseen by Captains. Commands barked out through loudspeakers whenever someone fucked up. In the far distance, helicopters boomed as Airborne Brigade practiced drills. A group of Legionnaires jogged past, all nodding in acknowledgement.

Axton assessed the Legionnaires as well as the Captains. His combat boots thudded softly as he walked down the dirt pathway, wearing black fatigue pants and shirt, gloves, and his helm over his head. Yells rang out as a Captain corrected a Legionnaire mishandling a rifle.

"When you lay flat on your stomach, you have to arch your back, rest on your elbows, and tuck it tight against your shoulder! And for Creator's sake, bend your fucking knee!" The Captain got down on the ground to show the male the right positioning. The hand opposite the trigger held the rifle up underneath. "You should know this already, Legionnaire. For that, you get to stay here, in this position for the next hour."

The Captain popped back up on her feet, nodding at Axton as he walked by. He returned it approvingly.

She turned back to the rifle unit. "Fire!"

The cracks of bullets flying was like music to his ears.

"Are you green, Lieutenant? You fight like you're green!" The sound of Michael's bark turned Axton's attention to a muddy sparring area.

Both he and the Demon he was yelling at were muddied up.

The Demon sported a black eye that surrounded his thin-pupiled, yellow eyes and a split lip, while Michael only had a minimal amount of splatter on his clothes. The sight of Michael had Axton bristling, bringing his thoughts back to what Sarandiel told him of their time together.

"N-no! I'm not green, sir!" The Lieutenant sounded unsure of himself, pulling Axton out of his thoughts.

"What's going on here, General?" he said, voice deeper due to the helm.

The Angel turned to him with a sigh. All business. Personal shit aside.

"Lieutenant Ira has been lazy. Clearly not following his regimen. Instead, he was caught drinking and having the time of his life." He slapped the Demon upside his head, making him wince. "Why have you been eating mud today, Lieutenant?"

"Because I fucked up."

"More than that. Why else?" Michael crossed his tanned arms, black shirt fitting him like a glove.

The Demon sighed. "Because I thought I could train with a hangover."

Michael grabbed Ira by his shirt collar, hooking his foot behind the Demon's ankles, effectively laying him out in the mud.

"And what did you learn today?" He placed his black combat boot on the male's stomach, pressing down enough to knock the wind out of him.

"That I was wrong." Lieutenant Ira took a long inhale as Michael removed his foot.

"It doesn't matter what you think you know. It doesn't matter how good you are. You never come to training ill-prepared. If you're going to get fucked up, then you can be dishonorably discharged and fuck off. Is that what you want?" Michael asked as he held a hand out to lift the Demon back to his feet.

Axton hated to admit that despite how he felt about the Angel, he was a damn good General. Fucking bellend.

"No, Sir," Ira said, standing straight.

"Take ten laps," Michael said, patting the Lieutenant on the shoulder.

"Everything proceeding well, General?" Axton's voice rumbled through his helm. He motioned with his head for Michael to walk with him, continuing his assessment of all the various units. They came upon a unit of two dozen boots, fresh Legionnaires straight out of cadet academy.

"Yes, sir. The Legion is prepared and ready should a need arise." The Angel nodded to the group of trainees. "These boots are our recruits for the Quasar Taskforce." Being the most elite of the Legionnaires, Quasar Rangers worked the most dangerous assignments across the realms, going undercover and gathering intel, and bringing in those that needed punishment. "However..."

Axton could practically feel the frustration wafting from his General. He grinned under his helm, knowing he made boot training Michael's personal form of torture. The boots weren't an issue. It was a *General* having to do the job rather than a Captain that was.

"What is it, Michael?" He looked at the group and his gaze snagged on four particular boots. One of them had a shit-eating grin on his face while the other three seemed to crowd close, as if he was their leader.

"This one here is Gaelen's Demi, Mikal." The smile on the Demi's face dropped when he saw Axton. "I was preparing to teach him and his friends the same lesson I taught Lieutenant Ira." He snapped his fingers, pointing to the center of the sand pit in front of them. "Center."

Before Mikal could move, Axton held up his hand.

"Do you understand the importance of being a Quasar Ranger?" he said to the group.

"Yes, sir!" they said in unison.

"Do you understand that you are just a *boot*? You are nowhere near taking on the role of being a Ranger, and there is no guarantee that you ever will. Do you know why?" Axton looked at Mikal, who blanched. "I am asking you a question, boot. Why is it that you are not guaranteed that position?"

"Because..." the Demi cleared his throat. "Because we could die during training."

"And do you know why recruits die during training?" Axton drawled. Mikal stayed silent. "Boot, answer me." Axton sighed when the Demi shook his head in answer. "Did Galaen teach you nothing?"

You'd think the Deity of the Hunt would do better than that. He thought to himself. Another boot raised her hand, golden hair up in a tight bun. Axton nodded.

"Because they were too cocky." She gave a pointed glare at Mikal who returned it in kind.

"There are twenty-four of you here, and only twelve graduates. Whether you live or die to reach graduation," Axton shrugged, "Is on you."

He nodded to Michael and pointed to the sandpit. The Angel's jaw clenched as he moved into its center. "Lesson one, never assume you're the best." He rounded the pit, Michael countering him, fists up.*

"Take our General as an example. He's good. He's a general for a reason."

Michael went on the offensive, throwing a punch aimed for Axton's gut. He blocked and returned a jab that made the Angel's head snap back. The General narrowed his eyes, they flashed bright emerald. Taking Axton by surprise, Michael ran and speared him, locking his hands around Axton's waist. The male had reach, Axton had to give him that.

"Anyone, however—even me—can be taken to the ground," he said with a huff, before elbowing Michael in the gut to keep him from locking an arm around his neck.

Axton was holding back his hits, knowing that if he laid a true one, the Angel would have been dead. Fuck, he wanted to kill him for what he did to Sarandiel. But he made a promise. They grappled, sand kicking up into the air and covering them both. The General wrapped his legs around one of Axton's, arms locked around his ankle. The Angel made the mistake of leaving his side unguarded, so Axton pivoted and laid a punch, making Michael bark out a sound of pain and let go.

♪ "Something to Hide" by grandson

Axton kicked back onto his feet, hauling the heaving Michael up by his collar. The General drew up his knee, connecting with Axton's chest and making him let the Angel go. The helm clanged around his head when Michael's boot collided with it. Michael couldn't hide his grin of satisfaction. He was putting up one hell of a fight, and Axton had to respect that.

"But if you get too overconfident—" Catching him off guard, Axton snatched Michael by the throat.

"Fuck..." the General said through gritted teeth. Emerald eyes flaring as he narrowed them on Axton.

"Like I was saying, if you get too overconfident, it makes you sloppy. And when you are sloppy, you run the risk of not only getting yourself killed, but your team as well." He let go of Michael abruptly, who stumbled a few steps before righting himself. "Never. assume you're the best person in the room." His gaze slid to Michael. "And never assume you're safe."

The slight widening of the Angel's eyes let him know that the threat was understood.

Axton turned back to the boots. "Cut the bullshit and get it together. Act like a fucking team. Hopefully I'll see you all at the end of it alive whether you graduate or not."

"Yes, sir!" They saluted in unison.

"Return to your training." Axton patted Michael's shoulder harder than he should've. Oh well. Fuck him. "I'd like for you to oversee their training." The Angel opened his mouth to complain when Axton raised a hand. "You can and you are going to. Give a captain the minor assignments. This group has promise, whether you see it or not."

Michael nodded, wisely keeping his mouth shut. "Right. Thank you for the workout, General."

Axton grinned behind his helm as he turned and jogged off the field, making his way to the indoor Legion facility.

Axton smelled her almond and coconut scent before he saw her. His vixen. Immediately his cock woke up, ichor still pounding through him from laying Michael out. As he rounded the hallway, he almost stopped walking, drinking her in.

Sarandiel wore a teal off the shoulder blouse and tight white skinny jeans. Her heels clicked as she kept her eyes on a binder assignment she was reviewing. Fuck, she was beautiful. He stalked toward her, and she looked up before Axton grabbed her by the elbows and phased them to a weapons closet before anyone could see.

"Axton!" Sarandiel yelped as he pulled her in, palming her ass and grinding his erection against her stomach. She smirked as she looked up at him in his helm. "Well, that's sexy."

He chuckled.

"Have I ever told you just how horny fighting and training makes me?" he mused as his hands roamed, one sliding between her legs from behind. "That, and beating up my vixen's ex."

She gasped, slapping his chest.*

"You didn't! Axton, I told you—" Her words were cut off as he slid his hand under her shirt and palmed one of her breasts, making her moan. His fingers grazed over her hardening nipples that were covered by a sheer lace bra. The way her body responded to his made his cock ache. "Wait. Anyone could walk in." She moaned softly when he pinched her hardened nipple.

"I don't give a single fuck," his growl vibrated through his body.

"But the legionnaires. Mich—" she bit back a cry when he smacked her ass.

"Do. Not. Say that wanker's name. Let him see what's no longer his and what is all mine. We'll just have to be quiet, love." He glided the back of his free hand down her cheek.

Panting with desire, Sarandiel put her hands up so that he could remove her shirt. He ripped the bra from her, pinching the buds tightly. She whimpered, her shadows running up his shirt to flick his pierced nipples.

"Fuck, I need to be inside you right now," he growled under his helm. When he went to remove it, she grabbed his wrists, her eyes lidded with desire.

"No. Leave it on," she said, voice husky. His dick jumped,

---

getting harder as she worked on his belt. "I want to pleasure my devastating warrior."

She dropped to her knees, pulling him out. Licking her lips, she ran her tongue up the length of his cock, sucking the head slowly. Sarandiel's gaze seared through him despite having his helm on. She took him in her mouth, inch by inch, making him growl in the process.

"Shit, vixen." He tangled his hand in her braids, thrusting his hips.

She made a pleased hum as she bobbed in time with his movements. Shadows tore his shirt, leaving it in tatters on the floor before whispering along his glacial skin.

"Needy, as always, aren't we?" His voice rasped deeply through the helm. "Oh shit." He leaned his head back as she sucked him harder, tendrils of shadows wrapping around his balls with a squeeze, and more pulling at the bars pierced through his nipples.

Desire didn't even begin to cover what he felt. It was need, addiction. It was feral, animalistic. Magnetic and gravitational, his pull to her was stronger than he thought possible. Two cosmic beings on a crash course to create a supernova of emotion and pleasure.

"You're going to make me come. Does my angel want me to come on her pretty face?" A rumbling desperate sound escaped his lips as she dragged her teeth along his length. Sarandiel whimpered her consent by gripping his balls tighter, making him jerk forward and hold her head down as far as her throat would allow. "Fuck!" He bit back a yell as he pulled out to cover her in his deep blue come.

"More…" His angel moaned as she opened her mouth to receive his pleasure. The Angel ran her hands over her chest and breasts, the come likely giving her a high as it usually did. "Please, Ax. Fuck me."

"Hmm," he purred deeply under the helm. "Look at you asking for permission. Such a good angel." He pulled her up, pressing her against the wall face first. Running his hands down her body, he unbuttoned her jeans and plunged his fingers into her wet pussy. "So wet for me. Fuck."

Sarandiel dropped her head back to his chest as she moaned while his fingers thrust in her.

"If you keep going, you're going to make me come," she panted as her core clenched around his fingers. Using his free hand, he wrapped it around her throat, gently squeezing, applying pressure just under her jaw.

"Then, come for me, vixen," he said huskily as he ran the nose of his helm up her neck.

"Fuck. Oh fuck," her cries strangled as she tried to contain herself from screaming. "Yes! I'm coming!" She yelled as he finger fucked her through the orgasm to give her another.

"Tut tut vixen, I told you, we must be quiet," he chuckled, pulling his fingers from her and pushing them into her mouth. "Do you taste good?" Sarandiel nodded, whimpering around his fingers. Wasting no time, he pulled off her shoes and jeans, and gripped her hips, making her back arch. "I'm going to fuck you now. Brace yourself."

"Please, Axton," she whined, swaying her hips and showing him her glistening cunt.

He lined up with her entrance, pushing in slowly.

"Shh. Quiet now, angel." His voice was utterly dark and full of wickedness. He gripped her hips when she tried to push back on him. "Patience. Always so needy." Sarandiel let out a soft, frustrated sound as he continued to slowly sink into her. "Do you like the way my cock stretches you, vixen?"

"Yes. Oh, Creator above, yes," she whispered, shuddering as he sank in fully to the base of his length.

"Sarandiel, what did I tell you?" He pulled out to the head and drove into her with a slam, slipping a hand around her neck. "My name is the only one that escapes your mouth." He thrust hard, making her whimper.

"Oh, Axton. You ruin me!" His hand over her mouth muffled her scream as he tightly held her hips with the other. He hissed when her shadows gripped him by the balls in time with his nipples.

"Shit, you feel so good around my dick." Axton let out a deep grunt as he pumped into her, picking up his pace. Messy, wet sounds filled the closet, making him feral. "You sound so delicious as I fuck you."

Biting back a moan, he growled, "Bite my hand." As soon as she did what he ordered, he slammed into her, fucking her in earnest.

Axton let out a strained moan as her teeth sank into his flesh. As her core tightened around him, he gripped the bottom of her mouth while she used the top of his hand as a gag.

"Shit, I'm about to fill your sweet pussy. Come with me, vixen. Come all over my dick."

He could feel tears leaking from her eyes as she bit harder, managing to break the skin. Fucking her for all that she was worth, their combined orgasms crashed through them, rattling the closet, a few weapons falling from their mounts. Their bodies shuddered and trembled as they came down from the high.

"Oh, shit," Sarandiel said as soon as he removed his hand from her mouth. She grazed the bite marks with her lips. "I'm sorry."

"It's quite all right, angel." He rested the hand on the wall, silver ichor trickling down it, and bent over to place his forehead on her shoulder. "You take all that I have to give in ways I never thought possible, Sarandiel."

It felt as if not only were their bodies connected, but their anima as well. He didn't have the words to explain what it all meant.

"It's almost as if I was made for you," his angel mused.

The thought occurred to him more than once, but how could it be possible if Angels and Deities were forbidden to be together? Moving achingly slow, he pulled out of her. They both groaned, bodies trembling as their joint arousal covered their thighs.

At last, he took off his helm, navy hair matted to his forehead with sweat. He knelt, scooping his come up her leg to push it back inside her. She let out a quiet whimper.

"You will keep each and every bit of my come inside you…" he growled softly. Elongating his tongue, he knelt and licked every part of their remaining arousal from her inner thighs, occasionally slipping between her seam and making her moan. Smiling, he slid his tongue to gently rub against her clit. Her hips jolted and she swatted at him.

"Axton! Please, I'm too sensitive!" Sarandiel gasped, making him chuckle.

Standing, his tongue waved a circle in the air, gliding along her neck and making her shiver. He wrapped it around her neck while his hand cupped her sex.

'If you think you're sensitive now. Just you wait until you feel what I will do to you later.' Axton whispered through her mind before pulling his tongue away.

"You can be a tease," she scolded as she turned around to face him. He chuckled as he manifested a rag to clean them both. "Why didn't you do that at first?"

"Because I like the way we taste on your skin, love."

Sarandiel snorted as she put her clothes on and wincing when she saw his shirt. He chuckled as a new shirt appeared in his hand before he pulled his pants up. After putting on his shirt, he found her gaze on him. Their gazes remained locked as she pushed some of his sweaty hair from his forehead.

"You are so beautiful... just exquisite" He cupped her face and brought her in for a searing kiss. Her body melted into his as her arms went around his waist.

Fuck, he was getting hard again. Damn if he didn't have things to finish up.

"I'd devour you again if I could. But unfortunately, responsibility calls. I have more tasks to do."

"Ax! You should've told me that before—"

"Hush, my sweet vixen. They'll hear you." He nipped her nose with a grin, making her return it in kind. "I will bury myself between your beautiful legs again later. That's a promise."

She bit her lip and nodded.

"You always live up to your promises, devastation."

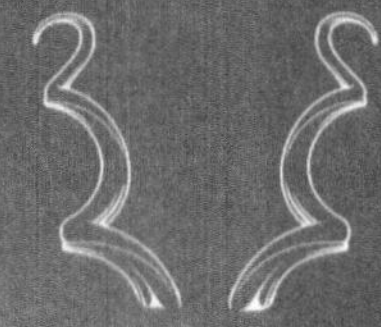

CHAPTER 13

AXTON

Two weeks later

Axton groaned as he worked through the assignments on his desk. He visited the anima Bethnal every week as promised. It drew out his need for violence and his body had been thrumming with aggression all day. He imagined what it would be like to make his angel beg. Sarandiel took all that he had to give, but could she handle this?

I'll find out tonight. He chuckled to himself.

Axton and his vixen were going to the Dalmiota Heights, an elevated archipelago that floated high in the atmosphere. Sarandiel was all he thought about. The way her soft skin felt under his hands, the way she took his cock, her brilliant mind. *Especially* her brilliant mind. He knew it was dangerous. Obsession grew from thoughts like these.

Suddenly his office door burst open, Tomis barging in like the chaotic fury she was. Axton's smile dropped as soon as she met his gaze. Her long, flaming orange hair floated around her, eyes bright swirls of orange and yellow. Her black pantsuit seemed darker under all the glow. Ever dramatic.

"Brother! I heard that you let the Demon council go back to their domains without punishment? Did they not keep those wrathful deaths from you?" She crossed her arms, glaring at him.

"Are you seriously coming to me *now* after a month and half?"

"I was busy. I was also only just informed! Why did you let them go?"

"Do you think I'm an idiot?" he asked baldly. "I wouldn't just let them go if I couldn't confirm who was involved. They can try to hide their lies, but *I* am their creator," he growled, annoyed by her presence. "It is clear Norrix is orchestrating the deaths."

The Demon tested Axton's nerves, plucking them one by one. He should've killed him centuries ago, if it weren't for his commitment to the welfare of all Demons.

"I have eyes on them. I need to uncover their plans."

"Fine." Tomis huffed, hair falling to her waist and the glow in her eyes diminishing. "And what of Aeshma? I am telling you, I believe she will break free. I must let my Chaos Wielder know."

Axton sneered.

"You do understand that if she breaks out, it means my Ascendent failed?" He shook his head. "No. It's impossible. Five thousand years she's been caged. You tell them *nothing*."

"Brother dearest, you must prepare. For *you* are our Legion Commander. If you are not prepared, then hope is lost for us all."

"Why do you underestimate me?" he snarled as he stood. "I *am* prepared. I am *always* prepared. Sarandiel advised me on having the Quasars do reconnaissance on Medius. As I said, I am prepared. I am not a fool."

"How dare you! I don't think you are a fool! I think you are incredibly stubborn and ignore reason," she hissed. "The prophecy the Demies wrote is enough of a warning. Even we can't change Fate." Her hair started to float again as her anger intensified.

"Fuck the prophecy. What does that trio of half Deities know of Euhaven? They rarely spend time there." He leaned against his desk. "Do not second guess me. Your Chaos Wielder will know when to show themself. Until then, we don't interfere."

"And what exactly are your plans *when* Aeshma breaks free?" she inquired as her anger tempered and she leaned on the desk next to him. Tomis was a head shorter than him, sporting smaller horns from her temples.

"*If* she breaks out, I have a contingency plan." He raised a hand before she could speak. "In addition to your Chaos Wielder."

Tomis took a deep inhale before sighing. She straightened

suddenly. Oh fuck.

"Brother, why does your office smell of sex and Sarandiel?"

"One, can't a Deity fuck a paranormal without question?" The realms were filled with different species. "Second, Sarandiel is in here every day. It should be no surprise her scent is in here." He kept a smooth mask of nonchalance on his face.

"Axton…" she warned. "You know that relationships between Deities and Angels are forbidden. You remember the last time it happened between—"

"I know, sister. We were there to witness it." He looked at his watch. "Are we done, or do you have more to badger me with?"

"Brother. Twin. We were Created together as Death and Chaos. War is what fuels us. I worry about you when you're in this state. Please tell me you're not…" Tomis gently took his hand. Her rich, yellow-golden complexion contrasted with his glacial skin.

Axton nodded, smiling gently.

"Don't worry. I will not risk us all." He lied through his teeth, no hint of it in his voice. He felt a pang of guilt lying to his twin, but Axton couldn't bear the thought of letting Sarandiel go. Not after having her.

Axton waited outside the compound, the wind blowing gently. It was late, and most denizens were in bed. Not a person in sight. He dressed casually for once, wearing charcoal jeans and a violet henley pushed up to his elbows. He yawned gently, stretching his arms above his head. The punishments he doled out earlier were weighing on him. Even if he took pleasure in it and quenched his thirst for violence.

"Well don't you look comfortable?"

Axton turned to watch Sarandiel saunter up to him. Great Creator, she was glorious. She let her silver and black braids down, falling to her waist. Her turquoise maxi dress complimented her dark brown skin and fit over her curves well. He smelled her arousal mixed with almond oil and coconut. Fuck, she was the end of him.

"Vixen, you look stunning," he murmured, not stepping too close in case eyes were looking. "Let's fly."

From between hidden slits in his shirt, great, ice blue leather wings burst from his back and gleamed under the moonlight as if covered with a dusting of frost. Sarandiel smiled as metallic silver and black feathered wings escaped her back, shadows swirling like a second set. They were just as stunning as she.*

Axton took off into the air, Sarandiel not far behind. The feel of the wind on his skin brought him a sense of bliss that he found nowhere else. He twisted in the air, bringing his wings in tight around him like a torpedo. Dropping a few feet, he laughed as he popped his wings out to catch a draft. Sarandiel swooped in next to him to do the same, shadows trailing like a tail. Her beautiful smile lighting up the night.

"So where are we headed?" she asked breathlessly.

"Dalmiota Heights" he said, hovering next to her.

"Really? I've never been." Her glowing black eyes lit up.

"For all the centuries you've spent in Orcus, you've never visited Dalmiota?" He was surprised. Most of the winged visited at least once in their long lives. However, tonight they were visiting a secluded spot where Axton was the only one with access.

"It seemed romantic and I never had someone to go with," Sarandiel said bashfully.

"Well, vixen, now you do." Axton smiled, grabbing her hand and tugging her along as he flew to the elevated islands.

He pulled her close, wrapping his arms around her waist. They gazed at each other as they flew, their wings instinctually keeping them aloft. Their lips found each other in a sensual embrace. It was slow and languid, a tasting of each other. Sarandiel moaned into his mouth, elevating herself high enough to wrap her arms around his neck and her legs around his torso. Axton gripped her ass, groaning at how it filled his hands. She suckled and nipped at his lower lip before plunging her tongue back into his mouth.

By the time they reached the Dalmiota Heights, they were

♪ "Heaven" by Pink Sweat$

panting with need.

"Vixen, we're here," he whispered against her lips.

Her eyes were heavy lidded, lips swollen from their kissing. Landing on soft violet grass, Sarandiel gasped in awe. Before them was a large waterfall made of turquoise and emerald stones. Rose colored water flowed over the cliff, the spray glowing from nearby bio-luminescent flora. He could live on her joy, the pureness of it in her smile.

"Wow. This is…" She took a few steps, wings returning to her back. Shadows played at her feet as she kicked off her shoes and wiggled her toes in the grass. "I don't know if there are words to explain this."

Axton walked up behind her, draping his arms over her shoulders. Her warm hands rested on his forearms as she leaned her head back to look up at him.

"It doesn't compare to you."

Emotion filled him as he turned her to cup her face. He planted a soft kiss on her forehead. Sarandiel shuddered under his touch, leaning into his palm. Words caught in his throat. How did he say all the things he desired to tell her?

Deciding to use his body to explain how he felt, he turned her and pulled her into a fervent kiss, moaning as she bit his lip and sucked on his tongue. Hands turning into claws, he gripped her hips, pulling her closer.

"I need you." Sarandiel moaned as her shadows tore at his shirt. Her hands traveled the expanse of his chest, stopping to glide over his nipples.

He bit his lip, moaning as she brought her mouth to suck on one of his piercings. Axton slid his knee between her legs making her moan as he ground against her core. Her teeth grazed his nipple making his cock jolt against her stomach.*

"Fuck, vixen." Axton groaned before snatching her dress and ripping it from her. He beheld her completely nude body. He dropped to his knees before her, staring up at her beautiful dark eyes. He hooked her knee over his shoulder. "You smell so sweet."

♪♪ "I Want It" by Two Feet

"Oh!" she moaned as the flat of his tongue rubbed her swollen clit.

"Already so wet," he growled before devouring her.

Sarandiel grabbed his horns as she gyrated her hips. Her cunt was dripping all over his mouth and chin, the taste of it like nectar. It was juicy and mouthwatering. He widened his jaw and thickened his tongue before penetrating her core. She cried out as she bucked her hips against him.

"Fuck, Ax." Her shadows flowed from her, ripping away his jeans to wrap around his cock. He moaned as she stroked him.

'Vixen, you taste so good. Keep fucking my face.' His words drove her forward as she ground against him harder, gripping his horns tighter. He ran his teeth across her clit and she yelped in pleasure. Sarandiel's thighs began to quake as she moved quicker.

"I'm so close. I'm going to come," she whimpered, more of her arousal filling his mouth, juices dripping from the sides of his mouth. The shadows gripped his cock, bringing out a deep groan.

'Be a good angel and come in my mouth.' Axton hummed as he thrusted his tongue deeper while applying pressure to her clit with his teeth.

"Oh fuck!" Sarandiel cried out, and he drank down every ounce of her come.

He dragged her orgasm out, continued to pump his tongue in her pussy. He gripped her ass, spreading them to glide a finger in between. She bounced as she came again, shaking as he pulled out.

"You make such sweet sounds." His voice guttural. Sarandiel untangled herself and dropped to her knees to wrap her lips around his cock. "Angel, I love watching as I fuck your mouth."

He moaned she took his thickness into her mouth. Her mouth stretched, hands wrapping around his shaft, before sucking him in as much as she could. She already proved to him how much she could take.

Axton lost all common sense as Sarandiel bobbed, gagging as he hit the back of her throat. He gripped her braids, fucking her mouth deeply. Her hands traveled up his thighs to grab his ass, encouraging him to thrust harder. Fuck, she'd be the end of him. She whimpered, breathing heavily through her nose as he drove his cock as deep as he could, holding her head before letting her up for air.

"Your mouth looks so good wrapped around my dick, but I need you. I need to bury myself so far into you that you will not know where my body starts and yours ends." Axton pulled her up, her lips puffy with saliva dripping down her chin. Grazing her lower lip with his teeth he murmured, "Will you take my aggression tonight, angel?"

"Yes," she panted without pause. Fuck, she was perfect. He bit into her lip hard enough to draw prickles of blood. It made his eyes roll, the taste of it like fine wine.

"You're *mine*." His need to take her intense. "You belong to no one but me."

"I'm yours. I belong to no one but you," Sarandiel moaned.

"Good, I'm going to prove it to you."

Axton's wings surged out of him. Hers immediately followed and they leapt into the air. They flew high above the waterfall, the flow of the water glimmering underneath. He gripped her nape, pulling her in for a passionate kiss. His tongue tasted her thoroughly and he groaned when her soft wings brushed against his leather ones. He wasted no time pulling her to wrap her legs around his waist and slam his cock into her cunt.*

"Axton. My devastation. Please," Sarandiel whimpered, her tightened nipples brushing against him.

"You're so fucking tight," he growled as his claws gripped her ass, drawing blood and making her yell pleasurably. Sarandiel's shadows whispered along the membranes of his wings, making him moan. "That feels so good. Keep doing it." He lifted and slammed into her as she massaged the sensitive skin firmly. His aching nipples brushed against hers and she whimpered.

"Axton, fuck me harder!" his angel cried out.

Growling, he shot his tongue out to wrap around her neck and pulled her close. Gripping tightly, he hugged his arms around

---

♪ "Make Me Feel" by Elvis Drew

her hips to hold her hands behind her back while he fucked her roughly and deeply.

'*So needy. I'm going to fuck you until you can't walk, vixen.*' Her pussy tightened around him, making him groan and pump into her faster. Sarandiel's legs trembled as she gushed her pleasure down his legs.

'*So fucking wet for me.*' Slightly loosening his tongue, he let her take a gasp of air before tightening it. '*Whimper for me.*' He growled through her mind. Body shaking, she whimpered. '*Do you want to come, love?*'

"Yes!" she gasped as soon as he loosened his grip.

'*Beg for it.*' Her juices flowed at his command.

"Please, Ax. Make me come. Please," she whined.

'*Beg harder. Beg for it like a good. Fucking. Angel.*' He thrusted with each word.

"I need it. Please, Axton! Please!" she sobbed in pleasure.

'*That's it. Begging looks good on you.*' Tightening his tongue, he slammed into her roughly. '*I'm going to come. Take it all. Let it fill up your womb.*' She bucked against him as he brought her over the edge while loosening his hold around her throat.

"Fill me. Fill me with your come," she screamed out before he came.

He held her body tightly against him, staunching the overflow of his come. Unwrapping his tongue, he kissed her neck gently.

"One day, you'll bear my Demi. I don't give a single fuck what anyone says. I *will* put a Demi in you. I will fuck, rut, and keep you coming while I fill you so full of my seed that it overflows your womb. Your stomach will swell, and I will worship you till the end of times."

She shuddered against him.

"Yes. Put a Demi in me. Please," she moaned against his chest as he let her hands go. "Fuck me again."

He glided them toward the top of the waterfall, landing softly behind boulders that kept them from falling into the water. Their wings snapped back in before Axton bent Sarandiel over the boulder.

"Does your hungry cunt want more of my dick?" he growled, slowly running the head of his length up the seam of her opening. She moaned, trying to press against him, but he held her in place with a hand to her lower back. "Well?" He continued to edge her, gently pressing against her opening.

"Yes! Yes! Please, give me your dick," she begged.

"That's it, love." Axton spread her legs further, slowly sliding his cock into her tight pussy.

He gripped her hip as he continued his torturous pace, making her curse urgently. The sounds of her wetness made him groan as he worked deeper. When he hit her cervix, she cried out. Shit, she fit him like a glove.

"I feel so full," Sarandiel gasped as he pumped into her. Her shadows flowed from her, wrapping around him. They pressed his ass to push him deeper into her. "Fuck me. Fuck me good, Axton," she moaned.

"Such a dirty mouth, vixen." He hissed when her shadows found his nipples again. "Do you like how hard I fuck you?" He thrusted deep, making her scream.

"Yes!"

"You should see how well your pussy takes me. It's wet and glistening. My dick driving in and out." Sarandiel clenched around him. His vixen loved praise. Axton stretched his jaw to latch onto her shoulder. She pushed her ass back in response.

'Fuck!' Axton growled through her mind.

While her shadows worked his nipples, more traveled between his legs to massage his balls. She gyrated against him, body shaking. Gripping her hips, he pulled her up to stand flush against him. Sarandiel's body trembled as he reached his hands around her, one going to her breast and the other slipping between her legs. He rubbed her clit while pinching her nipple.

"Devastation, pure utter ruination," she whimpered as she bucked against him. He bit into her shoulder, gently drawing droplets of blue blood. Her pussy gushed over his cock, making him moan and fuck her harder.

'Vixen, come for me.' Axton pressed on her clit before she

cried out with an orgasm that quaked the ground. Her shadows writhed around him. *'Let's play.'* He chuckled through her mind, knowing what she wanted. She whined when he disentangled himself from her.

"So needy. I'll not leave you wanting for long." Axton grinned, pulling her to the grass and hovering above her as he laid her on her back. He drove his cock into her before she could speak. She cried out, digging her nails into his back.

"Ah! Fuck!" Sarandiel's shadows slithered across his thighs, making their way to his ass.

He thrusted deep, pushing her thighs up for her to wrap around him. Shadows solidified, brushing against his balls before gently pushing at his asshole.

"I believe I made you a promise. I live up to my promises, when I'm through with you angel, you won't be able to walk." The wet sounds of his cock pumping into her made him wild. "You're mine." Axton growled.

"I'm yours." Sarandiel moaned before the shadows penetrated him.

"Fuck!" he yelled as she pumped in sync with his thrusts.

"Is my devastation, devastated?" She huffed a laugh.

"Such a naughty vixen," he chuckled.

Her cunt soaked him as he slammed into her, and she fucked him. The orgasm built at the base of his spine, his balls drawing in. He gripped her ass, spreading her wider as he worked himself deeper. The feel of her hardened shadows pumping into his ass made him see stars.

"Axton!" she sobbed.

"Fuck me hard, my beautiful angel," he groaned before devouring her mouth, tongue extending deep.

Sarandiel's shadows thrusted hard which made him do the same. She clenched around his cock, making him pick up his pace. He was so fucking close to the edge. He was overwhelmed with pleasure, fucking her as she fucked him.

'You are going to make me come, you fuck me so well.' Axton hummed as she responded to his praise. *'Come one last*

time, vixen.'

With that, they moved as one. He thrusted his tongue deep into her mouth while his cock drove into her soaking pussy. She fucked him harder at the same time. He pulled away from her in time to roar as Sarandiel screamed, their orgasms crashing through them in unison. Their bodies bowed from the force of their pleasure.

The entirety of the island shook from the quake they created. Axton's arms shook as he fought to not collapse on her. He retracted his jaw and laid soft kisses across her face. Sarandiel closed her eyes to the sensation, a satiated smile on her lips.*

"I'm yours," he murmured against her skin. He couldn't imagine being with anyone else ever again. Not after having Sarandiel. Her hand found his heartbeat, thudding wildly in his chest.

"You're mine." Her depthless black eyes gazed up at him.

He could've sworn she could feel his heart skip a beat. He kissed her sweetly.

"I love you."

The words escaped his mouth before he could stop them. Her eyes widened in surprise. Fuck! Love? Since when did Death feel love? It was too fast. Even if they'd pined for each over for centuries. He turned his head to the side, wondering what to say to recover. Her warm hand touched his smooth jaw and turned him back to her.

"I love you too."

♪ "Natural" by ZAYN

CHAPTER 14

SARANDIEL

"Sarandiel, do you have a moment?" Tomis stood at the open door of Sarandiel's office. The Deity was imposing, the chaotic energy around her swirling her hair in a frenzy.

"Yes, sure." She motioned to the chair in front of her desk, which Tomis promptly took. Her crisp navy suit barely made a sound as she sat.

"We need to talk about my brother."

Sarandiel bit back a yelp of surprise. Shit! Did she know about them?

"What did you want to talk about?" she wondered, keeping her voice steady.

Tomis let out a sigh, crossing her legs, red heels shining under the office lights.

"I need you to talk to him. He won't listen to reason when it comes to Aeshma."

Sarandiel almost sagged with relief. So, this wasn't about her relationship.

"Why do you think he'll listen to me? I mean, he said he was prepared, yes?"

"Axton listens to your suggestions. Did he not send a contingent of Quasar Rangers to Medius on your advice? Even if I were to say the same thing, he would never listen," the Deity grumbled.

Sarandiel almost smirked, thinking of their sibling rivalry.

"I believe you can make him see reason."

"I've spent time telling him that the deaths on Medius were not normal. I think he's taking things seriously in his own way." She knew with her whole heart that he was. Sarandiel motioned to the piles of assignments on her desk. "I plan to advise Axton to bring in more help on Mordax and Cassus. The animas are coming in too quickly."

"Good. That's good." Tomis nodded in agreement. "I've seen the state of Mordax. The Tenura is quickly filling." The Deity stood, sun bright eyes meeting Sarandiel's. "One more thing…"

"Yes?" Her voice was just a touch above a whisper. She had a feeling she knew what Tomis was going to say next.

"You risk my brother's position. You risk your life." Flaming orange hair floated around the Deity as her chaos rose. "You risk the protection of Medius. If Axton were to be removed from his position, lesser Deities will be quick to fill it. And none will be as perfect a fit as my brother."

"I am not sure…"

"Don't bullshit a bullshitter, Angel," Tomis snapped.

Sarandiel stood slowly. Would she fight a Deity and win? Likely not. Though she wouldn't want to fight her lover's twin anyway.

"Be that as it may…" The chaos around the Deity swiftly returned to her body as she moved around the desk to stand before her and took her hands. Tomis's hands were hot, thrumming with the chaos under her skin. "My brother is at peace, and I know it is because of you."

"How?" Sarandiel was at a loss for words. Had Tomis known this whole time?

"I know Axton. I saw a shift in his aura but wasn't sure until I saw him with you." She smiled. "Taking off into the sky together."

"Oh!" Heat quickly rushed to her face. They had assumed no one saw them.

"Don't worry. No one else was there. And I certainly will not report you," the Deity said softly. "I would not ruin his peace. But you have to be careful." Tomis let her go and pushed a braid behind Sarandiel's ear. "The world would be a dangerous place if Axton were to ever lose you." With that, the Deity of Chaos phased out of the office.

Tomis's words stayed with her as she wrapped things up and

exited. A thought occurred to her, guiding her sandal clad feet toward the hall of portals. Entering the gateway for Cassus, her dress flashed from navy to pale blue. Something had been pulling on her consciousness ever since her visit with Benécio, and she needed to find answers.

"Evening, Sarandiel!" A warm masculine voice drew her attention to the reception desk. The silver haired Demon stood with a smile, green eyes glowing.

"Kel! So glad to see you. It's been a while, yes?" Sarandiel said, returning his smile.

"We don't usually see you here at this time. Is there anything I can help you with?" He adjusted his lilac pollo as he sat back down.

"Actually yes. First, how are the new hires going?" she said.

"Surprisingly well. They understand the need and have risen to the occasion. We were able to onboard fifty new hires." Kel ran a hand through his gray, curly locks with a sigh. "I planned on reaching out to you tomorrow, actually."

"Oh? What for?" She pulled her holoport from her bag and came around the desk to sit next to him.

"We had three more animas arrive this week. Alchemists." There was true, genuine fear in the Demon's voice. "They all went Wayward before we could ask them any questions."

"Fuck…" she swore, wondering what this meant. "Any others? Even non-Alchemists that had similar symptoms?" Sarandiel let out a frustrated sigh when Kel shook his head.

"No. Other than the Alchemists, everything else has been as normal. Or as normal as things can get with the influx of animas." He gave her a look of guilt and it was clear he wished he had more to give her.

"All right. It's all right. Please pull up the gateway logs. Has there been anyone going in and out of Cassus that doesn't normally live or work here?" She typed away at her holoport, waiting for the connection from his holoscreen to hers. Logs and video feeds covered their screens.

"I've not personally seen anyone outside of the norm," he murmured as he scrolled. "Wait… there's a glitch here." Kel paused the feed, showing the brief and almost imperceptible glitch in the recording. "Is that even possible? How…"

"I've got it," Sarandiel said as she pulled a comm from her bag and placed it on her temple. Hologlasses covered her eyes as she dove deep into the files. She gave a small smile, knowing the Demon was staring at her. "I'm more than a pretty face, Kel. Who do you think designed the mainframe?"

As soon as the missing footage was recovered, she let out a stream of curses. Sending herself the files and deleting the ones on the record, she turned to Kel.

"Is that…"

"Yes. And you mustn't tell anyone. Swear to me on the Creator," she said as she hurriedly put her things away and stood. He nodded.

"Of course!" The Demon stood with her and caught her wrist. She lifted a questioning eyebrow when she saw the concern in his jade eyes. "Be careful. Please," he said softly. She laid a hand over his.

"I will. Remember, not a word."

With that, she rushed to the gateways. She *knew* a Celestial was fucking with the animas and records. It shouldn't have surprised her to find out who it was. Was he the only one? Were there more?

Sarandiel's head was overcome with the swirling haze of what she discovered as she exited the gateway into Novus Mors. She gasped when she almost barged into a solid, looming figure. Taking a step back, she took in the towering man in front of her. As tall as Axton, but as red as fire, the man was not someone she had seen before. His long white hair was stark against his crimson skin and black suit. His eyes were white with a deep red ring around the irises, and pupils of the same color.

"Sarandiel, Angel of the Night and Shadows, Creator of the Shadow Wielders?" The baritone of his voice sent shivers down her spine. Power leapt from him in waves that she'd never felt before. The more she looked at him, the more she realized he was covered in light etchings of Deity symbols.

Oh no.

"Y-yes?" Sarandiel attempted to take another step back but found that she couldn't. The sound of clinking had her looking down and finding cuffs around her ankles and wrists. She didn't even feel them!

No. Oh no.

"I am Apollyon. Seraph and Jailer of the Concilium Iuris."

A Seraph! She'd only met two in her lifetime, and they were both half-breeds. But she knew without a doubt that Apollyon was full-blooded Seraph. What were the odds that this would happen right on the heels of Tomis's warning? Would she be able to notify Axton? Without warning, Apollyon laid a heavy hand on her shoulder and the world went black.

Sarandiel woke in a bright white room. It hurt her eyes and she tried to blink away the dizziness that made the room spin. She found herself lying on a soft but uncomfortable cot and sat up slowly.

Closing her eyes, she said to herself, "Where am I?"

"You are on Sol. The Concilium Iuris will be providing judgment in one week time." The baritone of the man who appeared in the corner made Sarandiel yelp in surprise.

"Great Creator! Warning next time?" Head still fuzzy, she tried to remember the name of the Seraph in front of her. "A-a… Apollyon, yes?"

"That is correct." he said with a nod.

Her body trembled as a mixture of nerves and fear sat in her stomach like a stone. They fucked around and found out. Shit! She should've known better. Panic quickly overcame her, and she hugged her knees.

"Can you tell me what to expect? Why one week? Why not now? Will they execute me?" She snapped her mouth shut when the Seraph raised a hand.

"Peace, Sarandiel. You will go before the Concilium. They will hear your case." Apollyon's voice was gentler than she thought it would be considering his large and intimidating form. "They will ask about the Deity and who they are."

"What—"

"All that is known is that you've broken the Iuris by fraternizing with a Deity. Your name was the only one given." Apollyon's words were so carefully worded that it let her know the Concilium didn't know Axton was her lover. She could protect him. But...

Something must have shown on her face because Apollyon's voice rumbled, "I cannot tell you who turned you in. That is only for the Concilium to say. It has been a long time since someone last broke the Iuris. I can say it is a great sadness that you were turned in for loving someone unlike yourself."

"What will happen if I refuse to name my lover?" Tremors overtook her body.

"Sarandiel, I do not think it wise to keep that information to yourself. Admirable as it is, they will not show you mercy."

"I don't care. I will not give them a name." She shook her head knowing that she would do whatever it took to keep her devastation safe.

"It is time, Sarandiel, Angel of Shadows, and Creator of the Shadow Wielders." Apollyon's voice was like a balm as she lifted her head from her curled knees to find him standing across from her once more.

"Has it been a week?"

It had felt like one very long, tiring day. She thought she would go stir crazy, sitting in a white room for so long. They didn't give her any indication of the time of day, keeping the light on the entire time. Sleep was impossible and she could barely keep down the food they gave her.

"Yes. Please come with me. The Concilium is ready for you." The Seraph held out a large, crimson hand which she gratefully took.

Her body screamed at her as she unfurled from the seated

position she had maintained the entire time. Pins and needles worked through her as her limbs came alive. After steadying herself, she slipped her hand from his and followed him out of the barren room.

Everything was white. The hallways. The floors. Everything. She figured it was to disorient the prisoners. There were no windows. No way to indicate where she was other than being on Sol. She'd never visited the megastructure, despite having wanted to once upon a time. Sarandiel was led to a door that stood out from the rest. It was black with gold Deity etchings throughout. *The Concilium.*

"Please enter. They are waiting," Apollyon said grimly, following behind her.

Taking a deep breath, Sarandiel entered the… conference room? Where she had expected a large theater with the Concilium on some grand stage, she found herself in front of a large oak table with seven well-dressed Seraphs. Each of their seven wings were on display, ranging from black and silver to glittering white and gold. Three sat at the front of the table while the others were seated toward the back. Behind them was a gateway, bright and white. Was that for her?

"Sarandiel, welcome. Please sit." The Seraph at the head of the table motioned with his hand, encouraging her to do as he asked. With skin like alabaster and hair like midnight, the Seraph radiated power. His three-piece suit fit over a tall, lean body, and many silver rings adorned his fingers. "I am Matriel. Head Consiliarius." Her body shook as she sat in her designated chair. "Do you understand why you're here before the Concilium?"

"I am aware," she said softly.

"You've broken one of the cardinal Iuris." He stood slowly, resting his hands on the table. "It is punishable by lifetime in an Ascendant or execution."

She knew the Iuris but it didn't make her less angry.

"All for loving someone?"

"Not just someone. A Deity!" another Seraph said, glaring at her. She had golden hair that fell to the waist of her cream pantsuit. Her crystal blue eyes were stark against her smooth ebony skin.

"Zaphkiel. Remain silent," Matriel said with command in his tone. The Seraph clenched her jaw. "Angels and Deities are forbidden to fraternize. Do you understand why?"

Sarandiel crossed her arms.

"Why don't you remind me?" She wasn't sure where the boldness came from. Axton would've been proud of her if he could see her now.

"Watch your tone, Angel," Zaphkiel growled.

"Do you have a death wish, speaking to our leader in such a way?" A rich tenor came from behind her, and she turned to find the last Seraph had phased.

She didn't even see him leave the table. His grin made her stomach turn in discomfort; dark tan skin complimented by a cream suit. Did they always dress like this?

"I am Mitzrael. Consiliarius of Intelligence." He popped back to his seat, that sickly smile still plastered on his face.

"I will forgive you one time for a slight such as that," Matriel's silver eyes flared, lashing at her with his power. She fought the groan of pain that wanted to escape her mouth. "Angels and Deities do not consort with each other because of the devastation their offspring wreak on the realms."

"But there has only been one such offspring in history. How do we know it'll happen again?"

"Once was enough!" he snapped, lashing out at her again.

This time warm liquid dripped from her nose. She wiped away the navy blood with the back of her hand, grimacing at the agony flooding her body.

"If that offspring were to have completed their mission, Euhaven would've been destroyed! The rebellion surely would've made it to the other realms. And *you*, Sarandiel, made the grand fucking mistake of trying to do the same."

She blanched at his words.

"What do you mean?" she breathed.

"Did you think we were fools? Not only were you consorting with a Deity, you were planning a rebellion. A way to break the Iuris and leave it that way."

Sarandiel shot to her feet. "What? No! That was not my intention."

"That was not what we were told, Angel," Zaphkiel said with disdain. "A trusted source came to us to let us know of your plan."

"Name my accuser so that I can defend myself!" Her body shook as fury slowly crept up her spine. "I promise you, I am only guilty of being in love."

"The only way we can find the truth is if you tell us who your lover is," the Head Consiliarius said as he motioned to a circle near the gateway. "Stand there."

Sarandiel wanted to resist. She knew the closer she got to the gateway, the more likely she'd be sent away. But she was struck with the thought that if she was sent away, then Axton would be safe.

On uneasy footing, she moved to the circle. As soon as she stood in the center, a ringing pain shot through her. She couldn't hold back the scream that tore from her mouth. She sagged with relief when the pain rapidly subsided.

"Sarandiel. Who is your Deity lover?" Matriel stood in front of her, towering in his great height.

"I won't tell you," she panted.

The agony ran through her body again, making her cry out. It felt as if her insides were trying to come out of every orifice. Her organs twisting, body on fire.

"I will ask again. Who is your Deity lover?"

"Fuck you!" she growled. The protectiveness she had over Axton had been increasing the last few months, and it culminated to this point, right now. "I will not tell you. Torture me all you want, but you won't get any answers from me."

"Oh, we will," Mitzrael chuckled. "*They* might not admit it, but I have no problem with torture. I wouldn't be Intelligence if I did." The gateway glowed brighter. "Did you know that there are many methods of torture?" Deity symbols glowed, shifting into circles, before transforming into a tetrahedron. "An Ascendant is designed to drive the imprisoned insane. Most crack immediately, with the exception of a few. For you, seeing your lover die a thousand deaths would be a good one."

"This can't be happening! You are going on the word of one person, without asking for further proof?"

Mitzrael rolled his eyes, grabbing her bicep in a bruising hold.

Instinct had her pulling at her arm, trying to tear free from his hand. "No! This is fucking insane! Please. You can't do this!"

"Evidence has been brought to us. You were sloppy, leaving files of your contacts." The Seraph's grip tightened.

"What files?" She would be the *last* person to leave any information out in the open. Everything she had was kept in an encrypted comm drive, which told her someone was setting her up.

"Were you not talking with the Alchemist on Cassus? Learning about Aeshma's whereabouts to free her?" Mitzrael asked, ignoring her question.

"Yes, I spoke with him. But not to free her. He told—"

"Ah, so you admit talking with the Alchemist." Matriel shook his head, long black locks shifting on an invisible breeze.

"Yes but—"

"Are you aware that the Alchemist worked with a contingent of mortals with the dedicated purpose of experimenting on Celestials?"

"I found out after speaking with him. I tried to learn more but—"

She was cut off once again by the asshole, Mitzrael. They were not going to let her get a word in.

"And you tried to use that information to find Aeshma and free her," he said, sneering at her.

"No! If you'd let me fucking explain, I can tell you what the Alchemist told me!" she cried.

She'd definitely been set up. The question was by whom. The thought of her discovery in Cassus came to mind. She opened her mouth to tell them, but quickly snapped it shut. If she told them, it would only add fuel to the fire. They would assume she only knew because she was working *with* him. She was backed into a corner.

"We have no interest in your lies. We can reduce your sentence if you tell us who your Deity lover is. They are the only one who might be able to save you." Matriel grabbed her other arm, hold just as bruising as Mitzrael's.

She shook her head. No. No way in Orcus would she say his name.

"I *won't* tell you! Better to serve this punishment for something I did not do, than tell you anything." If she had to suffer for something she didn't do to protect Axton, then she would.

"Tsk." The gateway glowed brighter. "Did you know that time works differently on Sol?" Matriel mused suddenly, as if talking about the weather. "Time is a mortal-made concept. It is ever changing and never set in stone. It moves fluidly here on Sol. You never know how much time passes between here and the realms." He turned those glowing silver eyes to her. "Who knows if one week in the Ascendent is only a week on Orcus? Maybe only a month will pass while you're here for a week? Or perhaps it'll be the opposite?" He shrugged. "Oh well. I'm sure your Deity will assume you have abandoned them."

A sick feeling pressed against her throat, bile burning threateningly at the back of her mouth. The thought of the agony Axton would feel due to her absence tore at her heart. It was trying to shatter through her chest. She would be left bloodied and splintered into a thousand pieces.

As if it were in slow motion, she felt them lift her off her feet. She thrashed, suddenly very much afraid of going through that gateway.

Sarandiel and Axton's time together as lovers was only but a blip in the time span they'd known each other. She had to have faith that he would move on. Better to suffer in an Ascendant than risk him being in the same shoes. Orcus needed him far more than it needed her. All fight drained from her body as they brought her closer to the portal.*

"You will not get one word out of me. You underestimate what someone would do for the person they love."

She was thrown into oblivion.

Darkness covered her as she free fell. No matter how much

♪ "Lovely" by Billie Eilish, Khalid

she tried, her wings would not come to her. Wind pushed at her braids, whipping them into her face like lashes. When she finally crashed into the cold concrete, she thought her back would shatter. The pain that covered her from head to toe was beyond words. A sob barely escaped her mouth, taking breath was like trying to inhale water.

For a brief moment, she lost all feeling, and she nearly shuddered with relief, until the cold set in. Her teeth vibrated with the force of her shivers, breath coming out in short puffs of air. Maybe she would lay here forever.

"Love. I'm here," Axton's bass rumbled above her in the dark.

Her heart clenched as a small light illuminated from somewhere. Just enough to make out his solid hand and silhouette. Sarandiel could barely contain the sobs that overtook her as she grabbed his hand. It was strong, comforting her. Slowly, she stood up, and threw herself into his arms. Strong arms wrapped around her, and she inhaled the scent of frost and leather.

"What is the matter? Are you hurt?" His voice vibrated through his chest to her cheek.

"I... I thought I'd never see you again. I'm..."

Suddenly she remembered where she was. The Ascendant. So how was he here? Warm droplets splashed against her forehead, warm and sticky.

"A..."

She snapped her mouth shut. No, she couldn't say his name. He coughed, the sound wet and gargled. That's when she remembered what Mitzrael said. Fighting the need to look, she tried to pull away from him.

"What... What are you doing?" He rasped, more hot liquid spilling over her face.

No. She couldn't. Her eyes betrayed her as she looked up, meeting azure eyes that were quickly fading before her. Silver ichor poured from his throat in a clean line around his neck. Her body trembled as his hold around her loosened enough for her to escape. It was a mistake. As soon as she stepped back, his body fell and his head slid from his shoulders.

"N-no! Oh…" The horror before her truly stole the words from her lips.

As she fell to her knees, everything shifted. A bright light had her squeezing her eyes shut. The sounds of a busy Novus Mors surrounded her, making her open one just enough to confirm that she was indeed in the large city. Looking down at herself, she saw that she was dressed in the warm maxi dress she wore to Dalmiota Heights. No ichor covered her. There was no sign of Axton. How did she get to Orcus? What was the last thing she remembered?

"There you are. I have been wondering where you were," a deep masculine voice said from behind. It sent shivers down her body as she turned to Axton. He looked radiant in a violet henley and comfortable charcoal jeans. His smile made the butterflies in her stomach go wild.

"Well don't you look handsome." Sarandiel grinned as she approached before looking around. People were walking around and could see them. She let out a yelp in surprise when he pulled her in for a kiss and desire curled in her stomach. Pulling back, she took a moment to breathe. "Wait. We shouldn't be doing this publicly!"

"It is all right, love," he pulled her in again and she melted into him briefly.

The sound of a hovercar horn blasted, making her jump back before the car barely missed the both of them. Why were they in the middle of the street?

"That was close, A—" she stopped herself. Why was it important to not say his name? There was a reason she couldn't remember. "We sh—"

"Sara…" Michael's tenor sounded from behind her, making her spin to face him.

"*What* are you doing here?" she hissed.

"What you're doing is illegal," he said smugly. His emerald eyes flicked up to Axton behind her and a grunt drew her attention.

"Sarandiel…" Ax said, voice pained.

With abject horror she turned, nervous to have the Angel at her back but needing to see to her Deity. A large flaming sword had been stabbed through his chest. Michael's sword of old.

"No! A—" She coughed on the word. The Angel behind her chuckled as he moved to her side, grabbing the hilt of the sword.

"Say his name, Sara," he growled. "Say his name and I'll spare his life."

Sarandiel shook her head, the memory of the events leading up to now bombarding her. No, she was in the Ascendent. *Not* in Orcus.

"No. This is not real," she said with shuddering breaths as she watched the sword slowly pull free from Axton's chest. Ichor spurted, hot against her suddenly cold skin. Pain and grief surged through her, bringing her to her knees. "This isn't real," she said again as she began to curl into herself. Axton's body fell beside her, eyes lifeless. Sobs wracked her body as she rocked back and forth. "This isn't real."

"Say his name and you won't have to see him die for real." Michael's voice was too close to her, breath against her ear. She knew he was an illusion as well, all to add to her torture.

"No. This isn't real," she whispered.

And the cycle continued. Sarandiel watched Axton die a thousand deaths, and then a thousand more.

"This isn't real…"

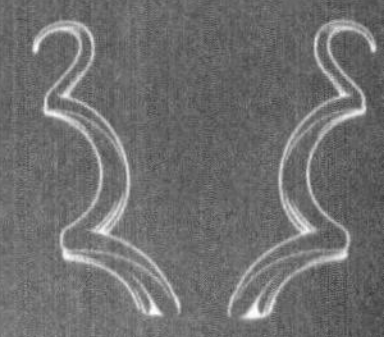

CHAPTER 15

AXTON

Love. Was that something the Deity of Death capable of? Clearly. Though it was baffling. Did he ever think in his long life that he'd fall in love? Absolutely not. But now, he couldn't imagine his life without Sarandiel.

The peace she brought, the joy of her laugh. Everything about her balanced him out. Her excellent mind was the most beautiful thing he ever knew. He couldn't get enough of his angel. His vixen. Just thinking of her made his dick hard. Fuck.

Axton shook away his thoughts and turned his attention to the binder on his desk. The rise in Cassus assignments added to his concern over the state of Medius. He was prepared if Aeshma was breaking free. He was *always* prepared. Most of the Cassus animas were in a state of denial. Their deaths were so sudden that often their processing through Novus Mors was like working through quicksand. He let out a sigh as he closed the binder, rubbing his aching temples.

"Dear Axton," came the sweet voices of Etis and Sortis as they phased in front of him. The double-headed Deity of Love and Sex had smiles on their faces.

"I take it you do not believe in knocking?" he chuckled as Sortis turned their head toward him, rose colored eyes glimmering with joy. Oh fuck.

"We are so happy for you," they said, turquoise skin flushing. "Love has found you!" Sortis's voice was like the sound of soft bells tinkling in a breeze.

"I'm not sure I know what you mean," Axton said before clearing his throat. Why did he even bother to put up a front?

"Axie! Come on. Don't play coy. The sex must be amazing," Etis chuckled, turning their lavender eyes on him. They raised an emerald hand to their cheek as heat ran through his body at the thought of Sarandiel underneath him. "Oh, it is!"

"Shut up." He tried to fight the grin that wanted to spread across his lips. Was he schoolboy? What the fuck? They were one of the few he felt at ease enough around to relax and smile.

"Did you think you could fall in love and we wouldn't figure it out?" Sortis said as they turned their face to him. "Are you worried because it's forbidden?"

"I beg your pardon?" He coughed, not expecting the question.

Yes, it was clear he couldn't hide his emotions from the Deity but *who* he loved was kept a secret. Or at least he thought it was a secret. Fuck.

"We know about Sarandiel. We've known from the first time you met," Etis said with glee, voice sultry and smooth.

Axton rose from his chair, concern growing in his belly.

"If that is true, why have you not reported us?" he wondered, containing his fear at the thought of losing Sarandiel.

"We would never get in the way of love. We are not like the others," Sortis said softly as they looked him over. "You have peace. Your aura shines." They raised a hand, smoothing it over the energy around him. It filled him with warmth and comfort and the knot in his stomach eased. "There is more yet." They smiled, rose eyes shifting to magenta. The color contrast with their turquoise skin was the perfect definition of love.

"Plus, the sex you two have is enough to fuel me for years." Etis snorted, turning their face toward Axton. He fought a groan and rubbed a hand over his face. They cackled as they patted his shoulder.

"You—" Searing pain cut off his words, the expression on Etis and Sortis's faces suddenly growing grim. His chest felt as if it were going to explode, the breath whooshed out of his lungs. "Sarandiel," he rasped. Something had been done to her. It was as if he could feel that she had been ripped away. No longer in Orcus.

"Oh dear…" Sortis said with pain in their tone. "Someone has done something very evil. I cannot sense Sarandiel."

Axton shook his head, pulling at his shirt as if it would alleviate the pain.

"Where is Gabriel? I know you can sense us all."

"Quasar Taskforce. Hurry, Axton." The urgency in Etis's voice chilled his ichor.

What the fuck was happening? He phased to the Quasar facility and stormed into Gabriel's office. The Messenger looked up from his piles of folders in surprise. He snapped to his feet, bowing to Axton.

"No, no time," Axton growled. "Where is Sarandiel?" The ache in his chest spread, and he was ready to take it out on someone. It didn't help that the Angel was identical to his twin, Michael. It only made Axton see white in fury.

"Commander, I don't know." Gabriel took a step back in reflex as Axton rounded the desk the desk menacingly. "What's happened?" The concern in the Angel's voice was the only reason he stopped short of snatching him by the collar. "Please trust me that I care about her wellbeing."

"If you did, then you would have been acutely aware of what your twin had been doing to her and stopped it," Axton snarled, making Gabriel stare at him with raised eyebrows.

"What are you talking about?" The Angel's voice dropped low.

"Ask. Him," he bit out. "We are wasting time. Do you happen to know where Sarandiel is? I do not feel her on Orcus."

When had he started being able to feel where she was? He hadn't noticed it before. They always happened to be in the right place at the right time. Had it been beyond coincidence?

"No, I don't, sir." Gabriel's body shook, from fear or fury at what he just learned about his brother, Axton was not sure, and didn't have the time to find out. "What do you need me to do?"

"Find her!" Axton bellowed. The office shook as a quake rocked the area. "Search the realms. Find out what happened." Pure agony shot through his system, bringing him to his knees. "She is in pain," he panted.

"How—" Gabriel let the question die on his tongue as realization dawned upon him.

"I need you to find her." Axton stood, despite the agony still coursing through him.

"I will do my best," Gabriel said with determination. "I will have Rhamiel and Michael—"

"No! You will not call in your cunt of a brother," Axton growled. "*I* will talk to him. Do you hear me?"

"Yes, sir. I hear you." It was clear Gabriel would honor Axton's command despite the many questions that must be swarming through the Angel's mind.

Pushing aside the pain coursing through his body, Axton phased to the Legion's training grounds. As soon as he saw Michael across the field, he appeared in front of the Angel in just one step.

"Commander Ax—"

"Where is Sarandiel?" Axton snarled, grabbing his General by the vest straps of his fatigues.

"Why would I know?" Michael narrowed his eyes but made no move to dislodge himself.

"I am not a fool, Michael, do not treat me as such. Drop the facade. I know about you and Sarandiel." The threat of violence was laced in Axton's tone. There was no mistaking why he was the Deity of Death. At the statement, the Angel shifted, instinctively grabbing Axton's wrists.

"What does that have to do with you?" the wanker seethed.

"You are dangerously close to true death," Axton growled as he pulled him closer. "Anyone under my purview deserves to be safe. And *you* have constantly made her feel the opposite."

"Is that what *she* told you? And you believe her?" Michael said through gritted teeth. "We're history. I broke up with her centuries ago."

"Where. Is. She?" Axton shifted his grip to the Angel's throat.

"I'm currently unaware of where she is," he bit out.

"Currently?" he growled, tightening his hold. He would have to address that statement after he found his vixen. "How simple it would be to cut your miserable little life, here and now." He watched with sick joy as Michael's face reddened. "If I find out you had a single thing to do with her disappearance, you *will* suffer the consequences of my wrath. Make absolutely no mistake, General. I will tear down the fucking realms to find her."

1 Month Later

"Lord Axton!" Gabriel's voice penetrated through Axton's head, adding to the already all-consuming migraine. Who would've thought that Deities could have migraines?

Before him, a sobbing Bethnal lay from the tongue-lashing Axton had given him. Literally. Said tongue was still in his hand after beating the anima with it. Work did not stop in Orcus and Axton found himself on Mordax more often than not.

He had been temporarily banned from Aether, having nearly destroyed it in his fury, trying to interrogate every Celestial he could find. Logically, it was impossible, but he hadn't been the same since losing Sarandiel. Tomis was the only one who could finally bring him down from his war path. Thankfully her power of creation allowed her to repair the damages.

Axton dropped the tongue before turning to Gabriel. The two of them worked well together, better than Axton anticipated. Other than being Major of the Quasars, they hadn't worked one to one until recently. The Angel was the complete opposite of his wank stain of a brother.

Upon confronting Michael, Gabriel found out the truth about Sarandiel and apologized profusely to Axton. There was nothing he could do. The Angel would have to speak to Sarandiel… if they ever found her.

"Have you found anything?" His voice was a disembodied snarl through his helm.

Next to Gabriel was a very disheveled Gaelen. The Deity of the Hunt's forest green hair was a matted mess, clinging to his russet forehead with sweat. His round brown eyes were sallow and bruises littered his handsome face.

"What the fuck happened?" he asked, motioning for them to leave the cell with him.

He pulled off his helm, tucking it under his arm. Gaelen's eyes were haunted, leaning on Gabriel as he limped down the hall.

"Seraphs." The Deity's tenor alto sounded strained. Axton froze in place, forcing the men to stop.

"Seraphs? The Concilium?" When Gaelen nodded, Axton let out a roar that shook the entirety of the Tenura. Pieces of the ceiling dropped, landing on the anima currently on the whipping stage. Others wailed, the sounds piercing.

"Quiet! Now!" As if flipping a switch, every last anima went silent at the command.

"Sarandiel has been turned in. Someone told them that she'd been in a relationship with a Deity," the Gaelen wheezed.

Gabriel's eyes widened as he looked at Axton from behind the Deity of the Hunt. Other than Tomis and Etis and Sortis, Gabriel was the only other person who knew of his relationship with Sarandiel.

"They don't know who the Deity is. So, they're interrogating each one that may have been close with her." Gaelen's eyes welled with tears. "We were only friends. She helped me when I lost one of my Demies. Rumors are spreading that she—" his voice cracked, not being able to finish his sentence.

"Thank you." Axton's body shook with wild fury as he nodded to Gabriel and phased to Dalmiota Heights, dropping his helm to the ground. It was the furthest away from the compound without leaving the realm, and the safest for his people. "APOLLYON!" he bellowed. Axton would be lying if he said he wasn't surprised that he hadn't been arrested. Why didn't they come for him?

"Lord Axton, Deity of Death, War, and Rebirth, and Creator of the Demons." The baritone of Apollyon was heard before the Seraph appeared.

"Where is she, Apollyon?" Axton barked.

"I assume you mean Sarandiel, Angel of Night and Shadows, Creator of the Shadow Wielders," Apollyon said calmly.

A growl reverberated in his chest as he stepped closer to the Seraph. They had always been friends, and met often to discuss Ascendents and new prisons. But at the moment, Axton only saw him as a potential threat. As someone who took his vixen and was a threat.

"Where. Is. My. Claimed?" The words escaped him before he could stop them.

His *Claimed*? Was that even possible between Angels and Deities? It would explain their attraction toward each other, the magnetic pull they'd had since the first night they met. Now that he thought about it, it had been more obvious than he realized.

Apollyon's eyes widened just slightly in surprise. "Your Claimed?" The Seraph was just as surprised as Axton. "This changes things."

"Yes, no kidding. Besides the obvious, why was she reported to the Concilium? I know there is something else. Why wasn't I called upon, having worked with her longest and being her superior?" Axton stepped back.

Apollyon cleared his throat, the compassion in his expression making it almost impossible to be angry at him.

"Sarandiel was not only brought up on charges for being with a Deity, but also for committing treason."

"Treason! Why the bloody Orcus would they think that?" The floating island shook as his barely contained fury leaked out, vibrating in his very bones. Trees fell as a quake nearly shattered the island, the land beneath him trembling as he listened to Apollyon's recounting of Sarandiel's 'trial'.

"She refused to name you. Even *I* did not know it was you. They forbade me to seek you out. I do not know why they did not speak to you about this." The Seraph sighed. "You should know that time works very differently on Sol. Sarandiel has been imprisoned in an Ascendent for Orcus's equivalent of one Sol cycle."

The consistent pain that Axton had felt since Sarandiel's disappearance made much more sense. What he felt was an echo of what she was going through. He vowed he would find the accuser and rip out their spine. It had been a very long time since he fed on flesh. Time was due.

Another quake caused a fissure to crack under his feet. He side stepped, the fury in him blunting all other emotions. With complete lack of empathy, he watched as the fissure tore through the island, splitting it into two. He barely registered the two halves breaking away while remaining elevated.

The sounds of surprised screams were distant, as if cotton filled his ears. Dimly aware of the falling debris, he threw out a net to protect those underneath until everything settled. Even in his anger, subconsciously, he remembered to protect his people. His body hummed with the surge of frenetic energy within him. The quakes subsided as he turned to the Seraph next to him.

Axton gripped Apollyon's forearm and demanded, "Take me to Sol."

With a nod and without question, Axton felt the world tilt. Deities could not phase to Sol, only Seraphs. If phasing was what someone would call what they did. Axton felt as if he was free falling, surrounded by flames that didn't burn his flesh. It swirled around him, waves of multi-hued reds, oranges, and yellows flowing before his eyes.

"Fucking Orcus," Axton gasped as they appeared in the familiar conference room of the Concilium. He absolutely hated the trip, each and every time. Righting himself, he looked at the Seraphs at the table, all of whom stared at him in surprise.

"Lord Axton. To what do we—" Matriel started before Axton charged at him, hand around the Seraph's throat, and slamming him against the wall. Before he could punch the wanker, a strong grip on his shoulders pulled him away from Matriel.

"Peace, Lord Axton," Apollyon said as Axton breathed heavily, body tense.

He shrugged the Seraph off, stepping away with a growl. Before a fuming Matriel could say anything further, Axton rose a still bloodied gloved hand. It was then he realized he still wore the gore of the animas he'd punished that evening. What a sight he must've made. *Good.*

"Someone tell me why my *Claimed* is locked in an Ascendent

of mine," he said menacingly.

"Your Claimed? We saw no Claiming mark on Sarandiel other than a failed one." Mitzrael said from his perch in the corner of the room. Funny how they knew exactly who he inquired about.

"The scar is centuries old," Apollyon's bass rumbled through the room. Axton turned to his friend, surprised that he spoke up. The red Seraph usually remained neutral and didn't stay in the conference room.

"Our agreement states that you are to speak to *me* before placing someone in an Ascendent. Yet you've not said anything to me about it, and I find that she's been in one for an entire month!" Axton bellowed.

The room shook, walls groaning. He didn't believe he had the ability to tear down the megastructure, but he knew he could do damage if he truly wanted to.

"Perhaps we should hear him out..." a nervous Agiel said from the far end of the conference room. Their golden hues shifted from Axton to the others.

"No. The Concilium still reserves the right to use Ascendents in cases of emergency," Matriel said without feeling, tone flat.

"For what reason was this an emergency? You took the word of someone with skeptical evidence, questionable at best, and decided she was to be imprisoned. It was overkill and you know it. Get her out *now*."

"Are you aware of *why* she was arrested for treason? That she spoke with—"

"The Alchemist. Yes, I am more than aware," Axton growled as he cut the Seraph off. "If you had deigned to speak with me *before* arresting her, I would have told you that she told me all about her conversation with the Alchemist, exactly what they spoke about, and the actions I took afterward."

"Either way, it still doesn't exonerate her from consorting with a Deity. With *you*." Mitzrael said with a glare. "Axton, we should arrest you for your relationship with Sarandiel." The Seraph smiled smugly. "Actually, Apollyon, take him—"

Before the sentence could be completed, the gateway

in the opposite corner glowed brightly. The room rumbled, the widening of Matriel's eyes the only indication of surprise.

"What is the meaning of this?" Zaphkiel said, eyes widened.

"*Axton, Deity of Death, War, and Rebirth. Creator of the Demons. Offspring of the Creator.*" A voice surrounded the room before a figure appeared at the gate. They were everyone and not. Their face every living being in the realms but not.

Axton and Apollyon dropped to one knee, while the others followed suit shortly after.

"Creator. The one of my existence. Of whom without I would not be here," Axton said with reverence. He'd only met his Creator one time, during the creation of his Demons.

"*Rise Axton, mine of mine.*" Though the Creator stood before him, the voice was everywhere at once. He stood slowly, keeping his eyes to the ground. "*You may elevate your gaze.*" Balm. That is what he felt. A soothing balm. "*Of the realms, we do not often interfere.*" Their nine wings fluttered around them, their body now formless. "*The Claimed are rare. When they are accepted by both, they are to never be separated.*" Rings like a halo shone above the space where their head once was. It was ropelike, intertwining with each other, moving rapidly. They opened and closed, showing the infinity symbol. "*We do not interfere unless such a thing happens.*"

"We've not completed it..." Axton whispered, though he wasn't sure why.

"*It does not take away that you two are meant to be Claimed.*" He couldn't be certain how he knew, but the Creator shifted their attention from him to the Concilium kneeling before them. "*Rise Matriel.*" The Seraph did as asked, keeping his gaze down. "*You know better than this, mine of mine.*"

He bobbed his head, like a petulant child being punished.

"The luris prevents Angel and Deity relations. There was no way to know they were Claimed."

Axton was temporarily blinded as what seemed like a solar flare burst through the room. Matriel was no longer there. In his place was dust and ash. Well, shit.

"*Rise, Mitzrael.*" There was no anger in the Creator's voice.

Not an ounce of emotion could be heard.

"Yes, Creator," the Seraph wisely said as he stood.

"Do not make the same mistake as your deceased brethren by repeating the Iuris to me. Do you understand the grave mistake you made?"

"Yes," he said softly. "We ignored Axton's demand to retrieve Sarandiel. We made the mistake of assuming Claimings were not possible between a Deity and Angel." Closing his eyes, Mitzrael's breathing shuddered.

Axton could smell the fear wafting from the Seraph. *Good.*

"A mistake that shall not be repeated. Just because it has not happened before does not mean it is impossible." The Creator shifted, the rings clinking as they formed an infinity symbol once more. *"Apollyon, rise."* The Seraph stood, head bowed. *"You stand here as Jailer of the Concilium. You will now also be Head Consiliarius."*

Axton could see Mitzrael's surprise from the periphery of his gaze. Apollyon nodded in gratitude.

"Make it known that Axton, mine of mine, and Sarandiel, mine of mine, are to be Claimed. No one will interfere." The voice surrounded the room before a silence covered them.

The gateway shined brighter. A figure approached from the other side, and Axton knew instantly who it was by the silhouette. His body thrummed with the need to rush to the gateway.

"We depart. Axton, please welcome your future Claimed."

Between blinks, the Creator was gone, the brightness in the room dulling instantly. He was at the gateway right as Sarandiel stumbled through and into his arms. Her eyes were haunted, staring up at him. Her white clothes were covered in grime, body trembling.

"Are you really alive? I watched you die. Over and over. They hoped I'd say your name. I never did. I never did." she croaked, tears streaming down her face. Axton nodded, pulling her close. Sarandiel gripped his shirt tightly, curling into his arms. "I watched you die..."

"Shh, my Claimed. I'm here. I'm so sorry I didn't find you sooner." There was a glow around them as he stood up with her in his arms. Sorrow followed by white hot fury filled his body, but he couldn't act on it. No, he needed to take care of his vixen. "We are leaving."

"Claimed?" she whispered as her head lolled on his chest.

Tears spilled from her eyes as she stared up at him with glowing black eyes. His chest tightened at the love he saw, at the painful relief that came with having her back.

"Yes… I believe so." He kissed her forehead before looking at the Concilium. "You will not see the end of this. We will revisit our agreement about the Ascendents," Axton growled before nodding to Apollyon, who was already at their side.

With his Claimed in his arms, they made their way back to Orcus.

CHAPTER 16

SARANDIEL

Two Weeks Later

"**A**xton!" Sarandiel cried out as she shook herself awake. Curled around her like a cat was her Deity, holding her close with his chest flush against her back.

"I am here, my love," he murmured sleepily in her ear, his chin resting on her shoulder. His bass soothed her instantly as she gripped the arm snug around her stomach. "Peace, vixen." Warmth radiated from his body to hers as he calmed her heart with his power.

While only a month had passed on Orcus, she felt she spent a lifetime in the Ascendent, watching Axton die. Knowing he was safe and snug around her helped relieve the ache in her chest. Her dreams—nightmares, really—made her believe she was back in the Ascendent. That the waking world was nothing but an illusion. Her memories leading up to her imprisonment were foggy. There was an inkling of something important in the far recesses of her subconscious that she couldn't bring to the forefront. Axton kept her grounded. He reminded her that she was no longer there.

"I love you," Sarandiel said softly, holding him tighter. Soft lips grazed along her bare shoulder, making her nipples harden under her cami.

"I love you too, vixen." Axton's warm breath played with the hair at her nape, making her shiver.

The Claiming hadn't been completed. They agreed to wait. But they also hadn't been intimate, despite her wanting to. She needed it. To know for sure he was really alive. But he wanted her to rest. He refused to allow her to do anything more than feed herself.

The Deity had been very doting.

"Ax..." she breathed as he kissed a line up to her neck.*

"Hmmm, yes?" he hummed, the vibration sending shocks to her core. Her back arched, pushing her ass against his growing hard on.

"I need you," she whimpered as he bit at the flesh below her ear. With clawed fingers, he ripped a line down her cami, exposing her breasts.

"I need you too, my love," he whispered as his fingers found her nipples and rolled them. A moan escaped her as she reached behind her to stroke one of his horns. "Fuck..." he groaned, grinding his hips against her, before extending his tongue down the front of her to lap at her nipple.

Slowly, ever so slowly, Axton slid his hand down the smooth expanse of her stomach. Blunting his claws, he dipped them into her cotton shorts and found her wet center.

"Oh," she moaned as he rubbed circles around her swollen clit.

'You are so wet for me, angel. Fuck.' His deep voice glided across her mind sensually, making her rock her hips back against him. When Axton thrust two fingers into her soaking pussy, she cried out.

"Please..." she whimpered as his tongue moved to the other nipple. Shadows flowed from her to glide over Axton's body. The feel of his muscled back, ass, legs, all of it sent sparks of pleasure straight to her clit. The fingers in her thrusted faster.

'Come, my love.' He growled through her mind as he worked her to a peak she didn't realize had been so close. Body shuddering, she held his horn as she came hard. *'That's such a good angel.'*

Using her shadows, she stripped him of his boxers before removing her own shorts. Her eyes rolled as she felt his cock against the roundness of her ass.

"Ax, I need you inside me. Please," she begged. As he pulled his tongue back, he used it to tilt her chin so she could look back at him.

♪ "Like I'm Gonna Lose You" by Meghan Trainor, John Legend

"Whatever you want. You need only ask once," he said huskily before kissing her deeply. While his tongue thrust into her mouth, he pulled her legs open, hooking an arm under her top knee. She moaned as he guided the head of his dick into her pussy. With one long and slow thrust, he was fully seated inside her.

"Oh, Axton!" she cried out before he captured her moans with his mouth. He rolled his hips, pumping in and out of her. She clenched around him, making him growl as he splayed his hand on her stomach.

"You feel so good around my dick," he groaned against her lips.

Her head fell back against his shoulder as she moved with him, gyrating in time with his thrusts. She could feel another orgasm cresting, so close to the edge, as she clenched tight around him again.

"Fuck, vixen. Come." He picked up the pace, moving his hand to grip her thigh tightly.

"Ax! Oh shit!"

How was it possible that each orgasm was larger than the last? It crested and rocked her, tremors lingering with each thrust. As quickly as the orgasm ended, another one overcame her, this time bringing Axton with her.

"Sarandiel!" he growled as he came, holding her tightly against him.

Their bodies shook as he unhooked his arm from her knee. They laid there, panting until their breathing calmed and their heartbeats synced.

He nuzzled her neck before murmuring, "I don't ever want to let you out of my sight, my love."

"If it were possible, I'd never leave your side," she said softly. Lazily, she let her fingers glide along his forearm, basking in the warmth of his body. "Axton?"

"Hmmm," came his response. She couldn't help but smirk.

"I never got to ask you… But where do *you* see yourself in five centuries?"

"Inside you, of course."

She could hear the humor in his voice and rolled her eyes, playfully swatting his arm. One thing she had come to love about him was his playful banter. If someone had told her a Sol cycle ago that Axton, Deity of Death and War, had a sense of humor, she would've called them a liar.

"Ax, seriously." She chuckled and then moaned when he rolled his hips, his cock still inside her.

"I *am* being serious, vixen." His arm around her waist tightened as he breathed a soft sigh. "The original goal was to take an extended holiday if I could convince my Demi to take over for a few centuries."

"Original? Is that no longer your plan?" She turned her head to look at him.

Axton kissed her cheek sweetly. He pulled out of her slowly to turn her on her back. The azure flames in his gaze stared down at her, love shining in their depths.

"That was before you, love. With your goals for Pax, it makes sense to do that alongside restructuring Cassus. The animas need better therapy and clearer separations by assignment level." He let out an embarrassed sigh. "This is not very good pillow talk."

"I didn't know you were planning to make changes on Cassus." She reached up to push a sweaty lock of navy hair from his forehead. His eyes closed as she traced his smooth jawline. "You amaze me more and more each and every day. That mind of yours." She grazed his forehead. "This heart." She rested her palm on his chest. "And—" Emotion constricted her throat, making it hard to speak.

"What is it, vixen?" he said softly, trailing his fingers along her jaw to the underside of her chin.

"I just..." she breathed, the droplets leaking from her eyes. "I've never felt so cherished and protected in my life. I've never felt so confident. And it's all because of you."

He gave her a warm smile, tilting her chin up so he could kiss her sweetly.

"Love, I am sure you had a hand in it as well. Give yourself credit."

"Yes. You're right. But you were the catalyst. Axton, I admire you because of the passion you have for your realm, for your people. It doesn't go unnoticed, and as I've told you before, it's the reason I stayed in Orcus. You've devastated me in the best of ways. But you also saved me." Tears fell freely. "You saved me from that Ascendent, and I will forever show you gratitude every moment that I can. I love you so much."

Axton cupped her cheek, staring into the depths of her anima.

"Sarandiel, I love you too."

Work. Assignments. Keeping busy.

It all mattered and helped her as she continued to heal. She wasn't sure when the dreams would end, or if they ever would, but remaining holed up in Axton's penthouse was no longer necessary. The week had been filled with investigating how the Alchemist ended up in Cassus and why they weren't told.

"I'm fairly certain that a Celestial is involved. Maybe more than one," Sarandiel said as she looked over the holoboard that held an amalgam of evidence that Gabriel put up in his office.

Norrix was front and center, their primary focus. Without proof, they couldn't do much but keep an eye on him. In her gut, she knew the Demon or someone close to him turned her in to the Concilium. The feeling was familiar, as if these thoughts had been confirmed. But if that were true, she'd have evidence.

"I'm inclined to agree," the Angel said with furrowed brows, assessing the information in front of them. The light olive Quasar shirt brought out the emerald of his eyes, and while she sometimes had a hard time looking at him, his energy was always comforting.

"Have your Quasars found any additional information at all?" she pondered, putting her braids up into a messy bun.

Gabriel shook his head, running a hand through his brown hair.

"They haven't. There are a few embedded in multiple governments and factions. We're at a standstill." She could tell the Major wasn't happy about it.

"All right. I'll check in next week," she said with a nod.

As she turned to leave, Gabriel said, "Sarandiel. Wait."

"Yes?" She raised an eyebrow in question.

"I wanted to say… Sorry." Guilt laced his tone.

"For what? You've done nothing wrong?"

"For not noticing," he said gently.

"For not noticing wh—" It hit her then. Michael. For not noticing what she went through with Michael.

"He's my brother. I should've seen it. I'm so pissed, and he's seen the end of my fist because of it. Sarandiel, I am so sor—"

"Gabriel," she cut him off with a raised hand. Stepping forward, she took his hand in hers. "Michael knew what he was doing. He fooled us all." Tears lined his eyes and she squeezed his hand. "I know you would've interceded had you known. Is it hard to look at you when you share his face? Yes. But you are so opposite him that I remember you are *not* him, nor will you ever be him."

Gabriel nodded, breathing slowly through his nose.

"He didn't deserve you. I'm glad you found happiness with Commander Axton."

"Thank you, Gabe," Sarandiel said with a warm smile.

She squeezed his hand once more before leaving the office. As she walked down the hall, a sense of love and lust hit her in the gut. She turned quickly and found Etis and Sortis standing beside her.

"Andi!" Etis squealed, their smile wide and bright. Turquoise eyes shined, adding a glow to their emerald skin.

She chuckled as she gave a nod to the Deity.

"Sarandiel, we are so happy you are well." Sortis turned their rose-colored eyes to her. "The love you share with Axton is beyond this world. We didn't know until the Creator confirmed it!"

"Confirmed what?" She inquired with a smile on her lips. It was impossible *not* to around the Deity of Love and Sex.

"That you're meant to be Claimed. It explains why the love

and sex you have is so potent." Etis winked, making Sarandiel flush with heat. "Speaking of..." They placed a hot hand on her shoulder. Her knees almost buckled from the wave of arousal that shook her from head to toe.

"What..." she breathed.

"You have some catching up to do. Don't worry. He feels it too," Etis's grin widened. "Incoming. In 3... 2..."

Suddenly Axton phased in front of her, making her yelp as he scooped her up.

"You're *mine*. I crave you right now."*

She could hear Etis's cackle as Axton phased them into his large bedroom, wasting no time crashing his lips to hers as he held her. She wrapped her legs around him and moaned as he gripped her ass. His fingers found her thong and tore it apart. Her need for him was wild. She couldn't get enough. Her tongue thrust into his mouth, tasting him as if he were her last meal. He groaned, the sound rumbling through her body.

"You're mine, Sarandiel. Mine only," Axton growled into her neck as he suckled and nipped.

She was feral for this Deity.

"Only yours. No one else's," Sarandiel moaned before he tossed her playfully on a bed large enough to fit ten grown Angels.

Her gaze ate Axton up as he took off his shirt, muscles bunching with the movements. His flaming gaze eye fucked her as he got on the bed and crawled to her. His jaw widened and his long tongue circled in the air as if tasting her from a distance. She could see all of his teeth and it thrilled her.

Oh. Fucking. Creator.

"I am going to devour you, my sweet angel." His guttural voice made her arousal flare. Axton's tongue wrapped around her ankle, pulling her closer. The delicious appendage writhed along her leg, sliding under her dress and finding her wet center. He hummed in pleasure, the vibration traveling down his tongue. Her back arched as he lapped at her clit, making her see stars.

"Oh shit!" Sarandiel cried out as Axton thrusted his tongue

♪ "P*$$Y Fairy (OTW)" by Jhené Aiko

into her.

He wrapped his hands at the crease of her thighs and pulled her closer. Her hands instinctively went to his horns, stroking them as she ground her pussy on his face. The Deity symbols lit up under her touch.

'Fuck, that feels good.' His growl rumbled through her mind.

Covering her with his jaw, his teeth pushed on her clit as his tongue continued pumping in her. She moaned as she undulated, gripping his horns tighter. She could feel her orgasm building, her cunt clenching around his tongue.

"I'm going to come. Fuck, Axton!"

'Be a good angel and come for me.'

Her brain short-circuited as she came with such force that her back bowed off the bed. The Deity rode out the orgasm, thrusting her into a second, smaller, orgasm. She panted as he looked up at her, his tongue licking her juices from his face and jaw retracting to normal.

"You have far too many clothes on, and I need to taste you," Sarandiel whined. She took off her dress and tossed it to the side as she rose to her knees. Axton chuckled as he took off his remaining clothes. She watched him hungrily as his dick was freed and nearly dove at him.

"So needy..." he huffed as she tackled him. He could've resisted, she knew this. But she loved that he entertained her and fell back with her on top.

"Shut up." Sarandiel grinned before kissing him, tasting her in his mouth. Axton moaned as her shadows brushed over his body, wrapping around his cock. "Do you like that, my devastation?" she whispered against his lips as her shadows stroked him.

"Hmm. Yes, vixen." He groaned as she gripped him tighter, his length hard and smooth under her shadowy touch.

"Are you mine?" His hips bucked as she pumped him.

"You own me, Sarandiel. I will receive whatever you wish to give."

His words made her heart clench. She loved him in ways that were beyond comprehension. She never thought it would be possible. Her tongue trailed his lips.

"Then open up." His eyes darkened as he opened his mouth. At first, she was unsure of herself. She knew what she wanted to do, but had never done it before.

"I'm yours. Prove it to me," he said gently as his hands trailed up her thighs to grip her ass.

"You're mine," she hummed before solidifying her shadows into the shape of a dick and slowly drove it into his mouth.

The sensations of his tongue around her shadows sent tremors of arousal straight to her core. Fingers having turned into claws gripped her ass tighter, the pain radiating up her spine in pleasure.

"Again," he growled when she pulled out.

As she did what he instructed, his hips bucked, making her yelp. He sucked on the hardened shadow, and it felt as if his lips were on her clit. She moaned as she pumped in and out of his mouth.

'*Shit, this is so erotic. Fuck my mouth good, angel.*' He growled as he snaked his hand between her legs and drove his fingers into her. With every thrust she made, he did the same. The sensations were overwhelming in the best way. Axton moaned as she fucked his mouth.

"Do you like that, Ax?" she breathed as she felt an orgasm nearing.

'*Fuck. Yes.*' His voice was a sensual caress through her mind.

"Maybe one day I'll fuck your mouth and ass at the same time."

The statement made him thrust his fingers deeper into her. She cried out as she came, her arousal drenching him. She pulled her shadows from his mouth, looking down at his blazing sapphire gaze.

"Yours. Forever yours," he whispered.

Warmth flooded her at the words.

Sarandiel kissed down Axton's body. She sucked in one of his nipples, tongue flicking the piercing. It was one of the sexiest things about him. He hissed in pleasure as her shadows rose to pinch the other. She became wetter with each moan he made, knowing that she was the one bringing him pleasure. Her shadows replaced her mouth as she continued her way south. His cock twitched against her as she slowly teased him with her body.

"Naughty vixen," Axton said as he put his hands behind his head to watch her. She smiled as her hands found his thick length. "Fuck," he groaned as she stroked him with both her hands.

"Do you like that?" Sarandiel said seductively. She gripped him as her shadows grazed his nipples.

"Fuck, yes."

She kept her eyes on him as she brought the lazuline head to her mouth. She licked the smooth velvet crown, bringing out a deep growl. It vibrated through Axton's body, making hers sing. Sarandiel wrapped her lips around his dick and sucked him in slowly.

His eyes flared, lips parted as he panted.

"Angel, you know what teasing gets you," he said as he reached out and gripped her braids. "Do you want to be punished or are you going to be a good angel and suck my dick?"

Sarandiel moaned as she took him in as much as she could. She didn't want to be punished. She desired to be good and give him every bit of herself. Axton bucked his hips with a curse, making her gag. Saliva dripped from her mouth as she continued to bob her head. He held her and thrusted forward, hitting the back of her throat. As he fucked her mouth, Sarandiel's arousal flowed from her core.

"Vixen, it's breathtaking watching you suck my dick." Axton's body shuddered, letting her up for air.

She whimpered at the praise, desiring more of him. Gripping his shaft tighter, she sucked harder. He instinctively gripped her braids as he lifted his hips to meet her with every bob. She could taste the mild saltiness of his pre-come and desired to have it cover her. Sarandiel pulled away from him with a gasp.

"Axton, I want your come on me."

Axton rose to his knees, pulling her up and gripping her braids to turn her face up to him.

"You want this come all over you?" He ran the tip of his cock along her lips. Her tongue snaked out and he moaned as she licked the underside of the head.

"Yes," she breathed.

Axton slowly pushed himself into her mouth before pulling back out.

"How badly do you want me to paint you with my come?" he growled, the tip of his dick glistening.

She knew he was close.

"So fucking bad. Please," she begged.

"Fuck, I love it when you beg. I think you should do it more often," he groaned before thrusting into her mouth. Keeping one hand in her braids, he used the other to grip under her chin. Keeping her still, he fucked her thoroughly. "Eyes on me, vixen. Watch as I cover you with my come."

She met his gaze and he yelled in desire, pulling out to paint her with his pleasure. Cerulean come shot out in jets, filling her mouth, covering her face and breasts. It glistened along her dark brown skin, turning navy. It dripped from her chin and the sensation had her body buzzing. Fuck she could get addicted to this.

"Hmm… I like you messy."

Oh, fuck he was going to be the death of her. He kissed her thoroughly, tasting himself on her lips and getting his own release all over his chest. Laying back, he pulled her on top of him, hovering her pussy over his length. His azure come was a contrast on his glacial skin and it was hot as fuck.*

"I need you." Sarandiel breathed, emotions swelling inside. "I want you. I desire you. I can't get enough." She cried out as he impaled her deeply. Her legs trembled from the full feeling. "Fuck!" Her shadows writhed along Axton's body, feeling every inch of him. He groaned, gripping her hips as she rode him.

"Now that I have you, I can't imagine life without you." His words were her undoing. "*No one* will have you but me," he growled. She nodded, bouncing on him. "Say it," he said as he bucked his hips.

"No one but you. Only you. Always yours." There was a tug of energy that pulled her to him. It spread like warmth from her heart,

---

♪♪ "Heavenly Bodies – Villains Overture" – by Arankai

traveling to meet his. "A Claiming."

Sarandiel gasped as his fingers found her clit. His tongue extended and wrapped around her breast, the end flicking her nipple. She leaned her hands on his abs as she fucked him harder and met him thrust for thrust.

'Hmmm, you feel it too, my angel?' Axton's voice was a caress in her mind. His fingers swirled as they pressed on her clit.

Her body jolted in response, the orgasm building inside. The warmth between them grew hotter. Surrounding them, she could see the flow of sapphire and black swirling together.

"Yes. Fuck, Axton, I feel it."

Tears of joy and pleasure streamed down her cheeks as he flipped her, driving his cock hard enough to make her scream. Their gazes remained locked as the energy swirled around them.

"Do you accept?" Axton asked softly as he slowed to a snail's pace, grinding his hips.

Sarandiel cupped his face, gasping at each slow thrust he made. All she saw was genuine love in his gaze. There was no denying it, and her heart felt like it would burst.

"Yes. I accept," Sarandiel said before Axton's lips crashed into hers.

He hooked one knee around his elbow, making each thrust deeper than before. He devoured her, tasting her completely, letting her know how he felt with such a passionate kiss.

"I love you, Sarandiel," he panted, driving into her faster. The Claiming energy overcame them, and her orgasm rose to the precipice.

"I love you, Axton," she moaned.

As his forehead rested on hers, the Claiming drew them closer, wrapping around their heads, connecting them mind to mind. Body to body. Anima to anima.

It was at that moment that their orgasms crashed into them. Sarandiel screamed as Axton roared, causing a quake strong enough to shake Novus Mors. There was a slight burning on her wrist where small Deity symbols of the Claiming etched itself, erasing the scar. One formed on Axton's as well. Emotions bubbled up and out of her as she sobbed. He cupped her head, tilting her chin up so he could kiss her sweetly. She felt droplets on her face and pulled back to find him crying as well.

"You've devastated me," she said with a choked laugh, sobbing subsiding.

"And you have saved me," he chuckled.

CHAPTER 17

SARANDIEL

"**R**elax, love." Axton's smooth bass rumbled, his hand gripping hers in reassurance as they walked toward the conference room.

Knots tightened in her stomach. It had been two weeks since they completed the Claiming, and they had been holed up, fucking like rabbits the entire time. The connection of their animas drove so deep that being apart was nearly impossible. They were visited by Etis and Sortis who told them it would continue for at least a Sol cycle while their animas balanced.

As much as Sarandiel desired to stay in Ax's penthouse and continue their marathon, business needed addressing and the realm needed taking care of. She paused as they got to the door, hands feeling clammy.

"I know a Claimed pair is of the highest decree, but only Tomis, and Etis and Sortis know we completed it. I'm nervous. I can be nervous, right? It's a big deal. What if they don't accept us? An Angel and a Deity? Claimings are so rare and—"

Axton spun her to face him with such force that it cut off her train of thought. Hands gripping her hips, he pulled her close, making her tilt her head back to look up at him. Her heart fluttered when he placed a soft kiss on her forehead.

"Sarandiel… Whether they accept us or not, we are Claimed, and I love you too much to be bothered by what anyone has to say." The smile on his face relaxed her slightly. "You are mine. I am yours. Nothing can change that." He took her hand again before pushing through the conference door.

"What in the bloody Orcus are you talking about?" Tomis's

shrill scream filtered out the door before they entered.

Pure pandemonium filled the room, making Sarandiel's stomach drop. Axton stiffened next to her, any trace of a smile now gone as he looked at the Deities and Angels talking over each other.

"What is all going on here?" The Deity of Death said loudly enough to quiet the room.

Eight sets of eyes turned in their direction. Michael's emerald hues flared as they drifted to their joined hands, jaw clenching in obvious anger. Etis and Sortis floated over to them. The double-faced Deity was draped in a pale-yellow silk robe, flowing as they hovered a few inches from the ground.

"Axie!" Etis squealed, making him wince. "I see you're official." Etis grinned. "Though I could certainly feel it. If you know what I mean."

Sarandiel giggled as Axton groaned.

"I am happy for you both," Sortis said with their lovely lilting voice. They turned their rose-colored eyes to Sarandiel. "I am glad you are safe and well." They gave Sarandiel's hand a squeeze before making their way back to their seat at the table.

"Well, brother. Before we go into the news that *Michael* just dropped in our laps, care to share the official news?" Tomis looked them over, making Sarandiel squirm internally.

Axton lifted their linked hands, their Claiming tattoos shining next to each other on their wrists. Soft gasps were made by Kutiel and Rhamiel, the former narrowing her eyes in question.

"Two months ago, Sarandiel went missing. We learned she had been arrested by the Concilium." Axton's gaze shifted to Apollyon who quietly stood along the far wall of the room. The Seraph gave a small bow of his head. "She was turned in for loving me. For seeing me for me." His soft lips brushed the back of her hand, making her shiver slightly. "For such an offense, punishment would've been necessary, but minimal. However," he growled and looked at Michael, whose expression was impassive. "Someone set her up and led the Concilium to believe she was plotting treason."

"No! Everyone knows she wouldn't," Kutiel blurted, Gabriel

nodding in agreement.

"Yes. *We* know that, but the Concilium did not." Axton waved his hand and shook his head. "We are still investigating what exactly happened." He let out an exhale. "As you know, the Creator let her go, because we were fated to be Claimed. As of a week ago, we completed the Claiming."

The room went quiet, the energy thick in the air. Sarandiel worried that everyone could hear her heart thundering in her chest.

"Well, it's about fucking time," Gabriel said with a smirk, ignoring his stewing twin next to him.

While Michael might not show his anger externally, Sarandiel knew him well enough to know he was absolutely livid inside. She gave Gabriel a smile of gratitude as his words broke the tension like a bubble.

"Great, moving on. Now let us talk about these Demons," Tomis said as she looked to Michael.

Axton's eyebrows raised in question.

"A legion of Demons are missing," the Angel said through gritted teeth.

"What do you mean there is a legion of Demons missing?" Axton's voice boomed, shaking the conference room.

She stared at him as he rounded the head of the table. Axton was incredibly handsome when he was angry. Blue flames lit brightly in his eyes, reflecting off his black horns. His strong jaw clenched, the muscle ticking. A scowl covered his face, his wide lips pursed in annoyance. She could feel the waves of anger coming off of him.

"Commander Axton, it seems to have happened right under our noses," Michael said, his tenor traveling around the room.

His emerald eyes held Sarandiel's, making her look away in irritation. Tomis slammed her hand on the table, cracking it. Her wild orange hair floated around her as she glared at Sarandiel and Axton. Chaos oozed off her, working everyone up.

"*You* fucked up." Tomis pointed at her twin. "You said you were prepared. How could this have happened?"

"By all means, dear sister, run Orcus, manage the thousands

of animas that come through each day, give out the assignments, and don't forget to make sure our Legionnaires are trained. Maybe you'll learn how *impossible* it is to know every last thing that happens in this realm!" Axton snarled.

"Angels are missing from Aether too," Rhamiel chimed in. His silver eyes glowed, making his umber skin seem deeper.

"What do you mean?" Etis and Sortis said in unison.

Rhamiel pulled out population records from Aether.

"The census doesn't line up. There are hundreds missing."

Everyone looked at Tomis, whose flaming hair lowered. Aether was the Deity's domain.

"Have anything to say, sister?" Axton snarked.

Sarandiel bit back a smirk.

"Fuck. It is Aeshma. I'm telling you!" She ran a hand through her hair. "I have to inform the Chaos Wielder."

"No!" Axton and Etis and Sortis said at the same time. Axton looked at them with surprise.

"No. We mustn't interfere. If Medius is doomed to repeat its actions, it must do so without us. If we intervened on every mistake the mortals make, they'd never learn. It would be a never-ending cycle," Sortis said as they turned their side of the head toward the room. "The triad of Demi-Deities have spoken. We knew this was eventual." The Deity's rose-colored eyes met every person in the room, wisdom and love filling them.

"So, we just let Medius go to shit and risk the realms?" Tomis scoffed, pacing the length of the room. "This makes no sense!"

"I have a contingency!" Axton snapped. Watching the twins' volley back and forth would've been entertaining if the realms weren't at risk.

"What does this mean for the Angels on Euhaven that have been waiting to live in the general public? Can they help?" Rhamiel spoke up.

"I am not so sure if I can rely on them. *You* and the others on this council were given the Ascendent to keep Aeshma imprisoned, but you fucked up and lost the bloody thing!" Axton snarled.

"The Quasars have been on Medius on a mission to find it.

They've been integrated into the mortal society. It is their job to find it. That is the most we can do at this point," Sarandiel said, surprising everyone in the room.

"Was this your idea Gabriel?" Rhamiel asked.

The Angel shook his head.

"No, that was all Sarandiel." He gave her a grin, making her glad they'd become friends again.

Tomis gave her a nod of respect while Michael's mask of indifference dropped briefly enough to scowl at her.

"Until the Ascendent has been recovered, Angels and Demons are to remain under the radar," Axton said, aiming to end the topic.

"And why can't you find it?" Michael asked with an arched brow.

Sarandiel bit back a gasp at the audacity. Axton's sapphire flames burst from his eyes as his horns lit up with Deity symbols.

"I am not omniscient. I don't know all nor see all. Neither of us are." He motioned to the Deities. "Only the Creator has that power, and *you* should know that. How have you been a General for so long?" Axton had a point, and from the glint in Michael's eyes, it was clear he was egging the Deity on.

She hated how no one seemed to trust him and his strategic mind. It didn't matter that he ended as many wars as there were ants on the ground. For the most part, she kept quiet to absorb the information being shared to consider in detail later.

Sarandiel could feel Michael's gaze on her again. Instead of looking away, this time she held it defiantly. If he wanted a rise out of her, he would fail miserably. Eyebrows raised in wicked amusement he looked away first. She let out a slow exhale, too soft for anyone hear.

Axton sensed her discomfort because he stopped mid-sentence to look at her, and then to Michael. His eyes darkened briefly before he turned back to Tomis to continue their debate.

"We *can't* change the fucking prophecy!" Kutiel yelled uncharacteristically, drawing everyone's attention. "We can't change what the Demies wrote. If Aeshma is to return, then Aeshma is to return. It is up to the Chaos Wielder to defeat her. It is up to them to find their Convergent. It is up to them to take up arms and lead this war if it comes to it." Kutiel bowed her head. "I must leave. The ocean calls. It is not calm in Medius. Time is getting near."

Axton nodded, giving her leave.

"Trust me when I say I have a contingency. We may not interfere directly, but that doesn't mean I'll leave Medius without a backup weapon to wield if the Chaos Wielder should fail." He eyed Tomis, who seemed to finally realize what he was saying. "Indeed," Axton said softly.

"Let's dismiss. We've exhausted ourselves here today," Sortis said, turning their side of their face to the room.

Sortis's rose-colored eyes shined as they looked between Sarandiel and Axton. Their bright teal skin flushed in joy. They gave a gentle smile before giving a nod and phasing from the room. Tomis followed suit, grumbling about needing whiskey, while Rhamiel left for the hall of portals.

"Sarandiel," the rumbling baritone of Apollyon captured her attention.

She smiled at him warmly. Despite having been the one to arrest her, he had been kind to her during her ordeal. It had been clear he disapproved of the actions that had been taken against her.

"I am surprised to see you here. The Seraphs have never been involved with the councils," she said, feeling Axton walk up behind her. Warm hands rested on her shoulders and she tilted her head back to smile up at him before turning her attention back to the Seraph.

"I am implementing some changes. We need to be more aware of the happenings in the realm, even if we do not deal with mortals directly. I will continue to attend councils going forward. Maybe one day soon we can talk about fortifying the Ascendents." The last statement was for Axton. The Deity nodded. "I will take my leave now." The Seraph phased out in a blink of white smoke.

As Gabriel and Michael bowed their heads to leave, Axton growled, "Michael, stay."

The Angel gritted his teeth as Gabriel left the room with a smirk.

"Yes, Commander Axton?" Michael said smoothly.

"Do not fuck with me. You do understand that I can end your life?" Malice filled Axton's voice as it deepened.

The Angel stuffed his hands into the pockets of his jeans, rocking back and forth.

"Yes, sir. I do." The lack of fear shocked Sarandiel. "But I also know you need me."

She stared at him, eyes wide. Bold motherfucker.

"That's your mistake; thinking your importance means more to me than Sarandiel. There is nothing I would not do to protect her or keep her from harm." Axton stepped closer to the Angel, eyes flaring with sapphire fire.

Michael looked her over before looking back at Axton.

"We established this, didn't we? I broke up with her. I have no interest in her," the asshole said. Ire grew in the Angel's emerald gaze. Michael might be an asshole, but he'd never been so bold to speak this way. Was he trying to get himself killed?

Sarandiel's anger rose, stifling any thoughts of concern. The Angel was a master at manipulation. The way he spoke as if he wasn't an abuser made her blood boil. Her Deity snatched Michael's collar, lifting him slowly from the floor. A small burst of fear emanated from the Angel as his chestnut wings snapped out, ripping through the slits in the back of his shirt.

"This goes beyond your supposed 'lack of interest'. I am aware of what you did." Ax held his wrist up, showing the Claiming mark.

Anger quickly replaced the fear that had been wafting from the Angel as he looked at the matching mark on Sarandiel's wrist.

"I don't know what you've been told, but I never laid a hand on her," he choked out before the Deity dropped him, causing the Angel to lose his footing and fall to his knees.

Michael quickly stood, brushing himself off and righting his shirt. Before Axton could say anything further, Sarandiel launched herself at the Angel, punching him straight in the jaw. Taking advantage of his shock, she grabbed him by his shoulders to pull him in close so that she could ram her knee into his groin. Michael fell to his knees again, a strained sound leaving his mouth.

"I am so fucking sick and tired of your bullshit lies!" she yelled, readying to kick him when Axton took hold of her around the waist.

'That was rather satisfying.' He chuckled through her mind.

She snorted, catching her breath, when he pinched her hips and moved her to the side. Grabbing Michael by the collar to bring him to his feet, Axton's eyes darkened.

"Let me make myself perfectly clear. If you ever try to speak to her. Look at her. Touch her. Or even try to breathe the same air as her without me there... I will end your existence," he snarled.

"Yes, sir. I will heed your warning," Michael said breathlessly, managing to keep the anger and fear out of his voice.

"Now, get out of my fucking sight. Go do your job, General."

The Angel bowed before leaving. Sarandiel wasted no time jumping up for Axton to catch her and wrapped her legs around his waist.

"You're so fucking sexy when you're mad," she murmured against his lips, licking them slowly. He groaned as his hands gripped her ass. "Take us home."

Axton phased them to his penthouse, walking them to his large bathroom. The bathtub was the size of a small pool, large enough for at least five Angels. He thrusted his tongue into her mouth, making her moan as she sucked on it.*

"Undress us, vixen," he groaned as she suckled on his neck.

Her shadows encased them, ripping away at their clothes. At this rate, they would need a new wardrobe every month. The Deity stepped into the tub and sat on a bench, water deep enough to go to his waist. It was blissfully hot and instantly relaxed her body. He let her go to turn her away from him. Axton bit the flesh of her deltoid when she whined.

"Let me wash you. Let me worship you."

Love rushed through her and she was overcome by the emotion.

♪ "Body" by Rosenfeld

"Ok," she said softly as he grabbed shampoo that smelled like sweet almond oil.

Slowly, he pulled her hair into a loose bun on top of her head, kissing her neck as he did so.

"You're so beautiful," he murmured as he slipped fingers between the braids to massage her scalp. As Axton continued to run his hands over her scalp, she found herself purring. "Does my vixen enjoy being caressed?" He chuckled as she hummed in delight. After placing another kiss on her shoulder, he lathered a loofah with coconut smelling soap.

"Stand my love," he instructed. She slowly stood, purposely gliding her ass on his hard erection at her back. "Such a naughty angel, aren't you?" He growled, dropping the loofah to grip her hips.

"I thought you liked me naughty?" Sarandiel yelped when Axton bit into her ass cheek.

He barked out a laugh as he let her hips go. Picking up the loofah, he glided it across her skin, raising goosebumps all over her body. He scrubbed her back, slowly working his way down to her ass and then to her feet.

"Spread your legs," he breathed along her skin. She shuddered as she did as she was told. Axton ran the loofah up to wash her inner thighs, purposely avoiding her aching cunt. Oh, the fucking bastard. "Turn, slowly. Let me admire your beauty."

"You devastate me," she whined in frustration as she slowly turned.

She rested her hands on his shoulders, watching him as he washed the front of her body. Avoiding her nipples, the loofah glided around the flesh of her breasts. Her back arched as he scrubbed her arms and brought the loofah down her body. With a firm hand, Axton gripped her knee and hooked it on his shoulder.

"We mustn't forget the most important part," he said softly, kissing her inner thigh and making her moan. Sarandiel gasped as he brought the loofah to her core, rubbing just enough to clean, but not enough to give her the friction she desperately wanted.

"Please," she begged.

Axton looked up at her, flames lit in his eyes.

"'Please', what, my vixen?" His voice dropped an octave as he continued to glide the loofah along her pussy.

"Taste me. Devour me. Worship me."

The flare in his eyes was exactly what she hoped for. Dropping the loofah, he gripped her ass as his tongue elongated. She would never tire of the sight of the navy appendage, and how it writhed along the sensitive spot between her thigh and pelvis. She closed her eyes to the sensation as it played along the seam of her cunt, gently rubbing and teasing.

'*Eyes on me,*' he whispered, making her eyes pop open and find his hot gaze. Sarandiel moaned as she watched his tongue enter her, reaching deep. '*Watch as I worship your pussy.*' She moaned as his tongue thrust in and out, making her writhe.

"That's a captivating sight. Watching how you fuck my pussy." She bit her lip, holding back a chuckle as he gripped her ass tighter. Oh, so she wasn't the only one who enjoyed praise! Axton's tongue thickened, filling her tightly. "Oh!" She cried as an orgasm built at the base of her spine.

'*You taste so fucking sweet, vixen. Come all over me. Make me drink it.*' He groaned through her mind as he pulled her closer and wrapped his mouth around her cunt.

His top lip rubbed against her clit, making the orgasm crash through her and flood his mouth. Sarandiel watched as he withdrew his tongue, her juices covering his chin. What a fucking sight. His fingers turned to claws and he glided them up her body. Gently he ran a blunted claw over her sensitive nipple.

"Oh, Axton," Sarandiel breathed as he kissed her pussy.

His free hand softly made its way to her clit, claw rubbing the sensitive bundle of nerves. His kisses deepened, suckling on her lips, tonguing her opening. He sucked in her clit before plunging his claw into her, making her buck against him.

"Scream my name and come again for me," Axton groaned against her as she took hold of his horns. He thrust in harder, using the flat of his tongue to press against her clit.

She was thrown off the cliff as she came.

"Axton!" she cried out.

Pulling his claw out, he gripped her hips, lifting her, and sat her on his cock. She whimpered as his thickness filled her.

"Oh fuck!"

"Moan louder for me, vixen," the Deity moaned deeply before sinking his fingers into the nape of her braids, pulling her head back and exposing her neck to him. She continued to writhe against him, riding him furiously.

"Axton. You devastate me!"

Her body trembled as his claws gripped her ass tight enough to lightly pierce them. The pain shot waves of pleasure to her pussy, making her clench around his cock. Sarandiel watched as his jaws widened like a snake, a thrill running through her, fear mixing with pleasure. He thrusted into her at the same time he latched onto her throat. Sarandiel whined, back arching, aching breasts rubbing against his claws.

'*Such sweet sounds you make, angel,*' he whispered sensually through her mind. His teeth bit into her neck gently, the sensation making her eyes roll. Her hands gripped his pierced nipples, tugging at them and making him hiss around her neck. '*Fuck! Keep doing that.*'

As she gripped him, he thrust his hips up, hitting her deep and thoroughly. Her legs shook as she felt another orgasm near.

"Axton. Don't stop. Oh fuck. Please!" she whimpered as he gripped her ass and rocked her on him. The feel of his cock going in and out drove her higher. She never wanted the feeling to stop. She never wanted to experience life without Axton, her Claimed.

'*Hmm. You know I love it when you beg.*' He growled, the vibration making her cry out. His tongue tightened around her throat, making her gush around him. Water splashed out of the tub as she bounced on him. '*Beg me to let you come.*'

"Please, Axton! Make me come, please," Sarandiel whined through the hold around her neck, clenching around him.

'*That's my angel. Keep fucking me. You're going to make me come.*'

He moaned, loosening his hold around her throat to flush her with a wave of euphoria. She sobbed in pleasure as she continued bouncing, his cock hitting her cervix. She screamed before he tightened his tongue around her neck once more.

'*You're going to have my Demies one day.*' He groaned, hands running up her torso and massaging her smooth stomach. Sarandiel whimpered at the thought and rode him harder. '*Come, my vixen, and take all of mine.*'

"Fuck! Axton!"

As his tongue loosened its hold, their orgasms swept through them, shaking the bathroom and splashing more water around them. Her body trembled as he disengaged from her neck, mouth returning to normal. Breathless, she flopped against him, head on his chest.

"I love you, my Claimed," Axton said gently, his own body twitching from the lasting effects of their pleasure.

Her heart ballooned, warmth spreading throughout her body.

"And I love you, my Claimed."

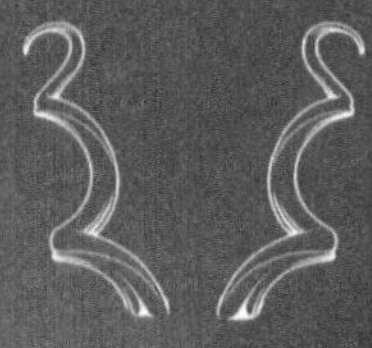

CHAPTER 18

AXTON

Present

Claimed and loved. It blew Axton's mind every time he thought about those words. The Deity of Death and War was not the best of company. How did he manage to find an amazing person to spend the rest of his life with? Who knew that his Claimed was right under his nose all these centuries?

He lounged on the couch, the HoloTV's screensaver illuminating the space in deep blues, purples, and magentas. His eyes were on the open balcony doors, watching the rise of Sol in the distance. Sarandiel murmured in her sleep, having fallen asleep in his arms. He looked down at her and smirked as she snuggled into the crook of his arm before returning his gaze to the sky.

The realms had been quiet these last few months, though dread still sat in the pit of Axton's belly. He knew it was the calm before the storm and he couldn't do a thing to stop it.

"How long have I been asleep?" came Sarandiel's sleepy voice. She sat up, rubbing her eyes. She could be so fucking adorable.

"A few hours. You did not get to see who the killer was." He nodded to the HoloTV. Sarandiel groaned, plopping her head on his bare chest.

"Damn! Was it the bartender? It had to have been the bartender."

"It absolutely was."

"I knew it!" Sarandiel's black eyes glimmered as she looked up at him. "What are you thinking about?" she asked softly, reaching up to cup his face. He leaned in and kissed her palm.

"The realms. We have done what we can. We still have not found the Ascendent nor the missing Angels and Demons. We still do not know who your accuser is. It is difficult to—" His words were cut off as Sarandiel rose to her knees next to him and gave him a kiss.

"It's no use spiraling, right? You've told me that a time or two." She sat back on her heels, brushing an errant strand of navy hair from his forehead. "Tell me again about that extended vacation you wanted to take."

Axton smiled, knowing exactly what she was doing and allowed for the distraction anyway.

"There's a realm in our sister galaxy, Ingens. The mortals of that galaxy assume Ingens is gaseous when in reality, under the dense orange and brown atmosphere, there is a full city. Much like Sol and Aether." He pursed his lips as he thought about the large realm.

"The mortals call the city the 'eye' of the realm—or 'planet' in their terms. They see what they want to." He shrugged. "Ingens has beautiful polar ice caps that glow blue, with luminescent skies during its evening rotation. I've only been there once or twice, but the scenery is unlike anything I have ever seen. Spending a holiday on Ingens would be enjoyable."

Axton pulled Sarandiel into his lap, making her straddle him. He could feel the heat of her core through her silk shorts and his lounge pants.

"I think you would enjoy it, my love." He kissed her neck, making her squirm. "Seeing those beautiful black eyes of yours staring up at the sky in awe, star gazing." He nipped the soft flesh where her jaw met her neck before murmuring, "Us fucking in a hot spring." Her sharp intake of air had him gripping her hips. "What do you say? If I can get my bloody Demi on board, we spend a few centuries on Ingens? Maybe make a Demi of our own after we've had our time?" he asked softly.

A Demi that he would make sure to not disappoint.

"I would love that." Gently, she took his hand and placed it on her flat stomach. "A Demi of our own would be amazing. Another piece of you in the universe, making it brighter." His heart clenched at her words, his fingers playing with the softness the silk cami. "I will go wherever you go, Ax. I'm yours. We share an anima. There is no me without you." Sarandiel trailed her finger across Axton's lower lip, which he licked and made her suck in a breath.

Kissing her deeply, he stood up with her legs around his waist.

"We might as well get the practice in. We'll be practicing for a very long time, won't we?" He gave her a feral grin which had her tightening her legs around his waist. "Fuck, I love you," he growled before devouring her in a kiss. He stalked them to their bedroom as they remained locked together, his erection now aching. He dropped her on the bed, making her squeak in delight.

They made quick work of removing their clothing before she pulled him to the bed. For a moment, they laid there, gazes locking as they faced each other. Their hearts beat in time with each other, their emotions intertwined. He knew she could feel his love as much as he could feel hers.

"Sometimes I can't believe you're my Claimed," Axton said softly. "I don't know what I did to deserve you."

"You didn't have to do anything. We were meant to be. I just wish I saw it sooner," she said equally as soft. "From the moment we met, you have always remained a constant in my life. Ax, I'm so damn happy you're my Claimed," Sarandiel said as she glided her fingers across his smooth jaw and down his neck. "Now… what was this about practicing?"

His dick jumped as he pulled her closer.*

"Hmm…" Axton's voice dropped an octave as she flicked his nipple.

Sarandiel leaned in and kissed his chest, wrapping a leg over the top of his waist. The scent of her already wet pussy wafted to him made him groan. Sliding his hand up her soft but firm thigh, he hooked her knee over his elbow. Sarandiel stroked his cock, rubbing the tip against her wet center.

"Naughty angel," he breathed as he sank into her. She

♪ "Crazy In Love – Remix" by Beyoncé

moaned against his chest, hands gripping his nipples. "I'll never get enough of you." Growling, he bucked his hips, driving himself deeper.

"I love you so much," Sarandiel cried out as he tightened his hold on her knee. "Give me your tongue," she breathed, turning her head up.

He extended it out to her, thrusting it in her mouth as he fucked her. She moaned as her cunt clenched around him.

'I love you, my sweet angel.' Axton said through her mind. She sucked on his tongue as she pulled his nipple piercings. *'Come for me, my sweet vixen.'*

The praise made her buck against him as her orgasm flooded her pussy. He pulled his tongue back and turned her to lie flat on her stomach, tilting her hips up to expose her wetness.

"You're mine, Sarandiel," Axton moaned as he slowly sunk in to the hilt. He took hold of her hands above her head, their fingers interlocking. His grind was deliberate and languid, rolling his hips and enjoying the sensation of sinking deep into her. The Angel arched her back, pressing herself against him as he moved. Gliding his tongue down her back, he ended at her ass. Using his knees, he spread her wider and elevated her hips higher.

"Oh fuck!" Sarandiel moaned as he lapped at her asshole. He pressed the puckering, making her jerk against him.

'Does my vixen like that?'

"Yes, oh shit, yes!"

His pace increased as he slowly edged her ass.

'Would you like me to fuck your ass with my tongue, angel?'

"Axton, stop asking me questions! Just fuck me," she whined as he teased his tongue in her, inch by inch, his saliva providing the necessary lubrication. He chuckled, causing goosebumps to rise on her flesh, and slowly pulled from her.

'So needy.'

The sound she made when he plunged into her ass made him buck against her, cock driving in deeper into her pussy. Her hands gripped his as she panted while he fucked her. His angel cried out as his tongue and dick thrusted in unison.

'Fuck you taste so good. The sounds you make drive me insane.' The growl carried through his body and across hers.

"It's so much. I feel so full," she whimpered. He pulled her hands to her lower back, gripping them with one hand while he wrapped his free hand around her throat. "Choke me. I'm yours. My life is yours."

'That's right, angel. You're mine.'

He tightened his hold as he fucked her in earnest. Her legs trembled as he drove deep. His angel. His vixen. His Claimed. She looked beautiful with her kissed swollen lips parted in pleasure, her eyes rolling from how good he made her feel.

'Is my vixen ready to come again?' He loosened his grip and she took a shuddering gasp of air.

"Yes. Yes, please, can I come?" she begged.

Axton thrusted roughly, his hips stuttering as he got closer to his edge. *'Come my sweet vixen.'*

Sarandiel moaned as he tightened his grip around her throat again as she jerked against him. When she reached her climax, he released her neck and the arousal came crashing down on them both. The wet sounds of his cock driving in her put him over the edge. Axton moaned as he filled her, come overflowing on them both. He pulled his tongue back, savoring her taste and let her hands go.

Obsession. She was his obsession. He massaged her shoulders before pulling out slowly.

"Open your legs," he murmured as she turned on her back. As she did what she was told, he ran his fingers up her inner thighs, catching their come, and pushed it inside of her. "Remember, all of my come stays inside you," Axton said before lying next to her and pulling her close.

They remained there, basking in the love they shared with each other. Just when Axton was about to doze off, instinct had him jumping from the bed. Sarandiel wasn't far behind, wrapping a blanket around her.

"Brother!" Tomis yelled from his living room.

Fuck. Axton searched for his lounge pants, sliding them on

without care for his boxers. He tossed his shirt to Sarandiel who quickly slipped it on.

"It's urgent! Put your dick in your pants and come out here, NOW!"

Axton ground his teeth as he stormed into the living room. He stopped dead when he noticed the black gore covering his leather clad twin. She looked like she had been fighting a battle, dropping two swords to the ground. Sarandiel gasped as Axton rushed to his sister.

"What the fuck happened!" He grabbed her by the biceps, looking her over to make sure she was unharmed.

Tomis shook him off, shaking her head as she paced, combat boots loud against the marble floor.

"We found your legion of Demons," she growled. "And the missing Angels."

A heavy feeling sank like a stone in his gut.

"Where?" he said in disbelief.

"Medius. They're in Euhaven. Aeshma has returned."

"Norrix!" Sarandiel shouted, gripping Axton's arm. Her eyes were glossy as if the memory just impacted her. "Oh Creator, I've finally remembered. Norrix was helping the Alchemists."

Well fuck.

TO BE CONTINUED IN

The
CHAOS
Wielder

ACKNOWLEDGEMENTS

Thanks to my friends and family. Your support means more than you know!

Many, many thanks to my alpha and beta readers! Holy shit, y'all helped me develop this story from a short novelette to a short novel. It has been your amazing help that got me to this point.

Thank you to the bookish community for their continued outpouring of support! Y'all keep me going each and every day.

To my ARCs and readers—my Chaotics—I love you all! Your feedback is invaluable and your reactions give me LIFE!

Thank you all for being with me on this Chaos Journey!

More to come…

ABOUT THE AUTHOR

A.E. COSBY IS A PUERTO RICAN and indigenous person obsessed with the dark and arcane. They are a bruja who honors their Ancestors and the path that have been put before them. They believe with their whole chest that they lived on another planet in another life. Being an Aquarius, this is not a surprise! Having vivid dreams of this world, they invite you to experience this planet through their dark urban fantasy novels. They share the darkest parts of their soul through their work.

A.E. is a neurospicy comic book nerd, enjoys sci-fi and fantasy, and tattoos. Ask them how many they have. (Hint: 14). They have three chaos gremlins and a husband who supports their dream.

You can connect with them through their website and social media channels.

hello@anissacosby.com
www.anissacosby.com
www.linktr.ee/anissacosby

CURRENT AND FUTURE WORKS BY A.E. COSBY

THE CHAOS SERIES
The Chaos Wielder
Wrath's Daughter
Blood of Fire
Storm's War

CHAOS COMPANION NOVELS
Death & Shadow

9 798988 659136